THE SHORTSTOP

To my brother, "Reddy" Grey,
to Arthur Irwin, my coach and teacher,
to Roy Thomas and Ray Kellogg,
fellow players and friends,
and to
all the girls and all the boys who love the
GRAND OLD AMERICAN GAME
—Z. G.

Text copyright © 1909 by Zane Grey

Foreword copyright © 1991 by John Thorn

Printed in the United States of America.

First Beech Tree Edition, 1992.

1   2   3   4   5   6   7   8   9   10

Library of Congress Cataloging-in-Publication Data
Grey, Zane, 1872–1939.
The Shortstop/by Zane Grey : foreword by John Thorn.
p.   cm.
Originally published : Chicago : A. C. McClung & Co., 1909.
Summary: Seventeen-year-old Chase relies on his talent and
inner resources as he struggles to succeed as a professional
baseball player.
ISBN 0-688-11261-7
[1. Baseball—Fiction.]   I. Title.
PZ7.G875Sh   1992
[Fic]—dc20   91-24034 CIP AC

THE SHORTSTOP

ZANE GREY

FOREWORD BY
JOHN THORN

BEECH TREE BOOKS

NEW YORK

CONTENTS

FOREWORD

Zane Grey is famous for his novels of the West and his passion for outdoor sport, especially fishing. He was a fabulously successful writer; his 85 books sold more than 100 million copies and inspired a staggering 111 films.

But when Grey wrote *The Short-Stop* in 1909 (the original title bore the old-fashioned spelling), he was neither famous nor successful. In fact, only four years earlier he had been a struggling dentist with one novel to his credit, which he had paid to publish himself. Three other books followed, but they achieved little recognition. Thirty-seven years old, despairing of ever making his mark in the writing trade, he tried his hand at a baseball book for "all the girls and boys who love the grand old American game."

The Shortstop proved a hit, going through three printings in its first six months after publication. Its success inspired Grey to persevere, just as hero Chase Alloway did in the novel. Over the next two years, Grey wrote *The Heritage of the Desert* and *Riders of the Purple Sage* (and, in between, another baseball tale, *The Young Pitcher*, which Morrow has reissued as a companion volume to this one). Grey's fame was assured.

Important as *The Shortstop* was to making Grey's career, why would anyone want to read it today? He wrote the book for money and cast it in the conventional pluck-and-luck mold of Horatio Alger and the Frank Merriwell series. What, then, makes *The Shortstop* more than a curio for the secondhand-book trade? First, Zane Grey knew how to tell a good story. He also provides a peephole into the past, an engaging view of ordinary Americans at work and play. Plus, *The Shortstop* presents moral dilemmas that are as relevant today as they were at the turn of the century; and for all its theatrical qualities, the book does flow from the experience and observation of Grey himself, who knew baseball as no other major American novelist has.

Mark Twain built a baseball scene into *A Connecticut Yankee in King Arthur's Court*; Thomas Wolfe recalled his boyhood memories of the game in sections of *You Can't Go Home Again*; Bernard Malamud, Philip Roth, and W. P. Kinsella set entire novels in the land of baseball. But in their youth, none of these authors played the game with such intensity and skill that they rose from the sandlots to stardom, in both the collegiate and professional ranks. Zane Grey did.

Growing up in Zanesville, Ohio, Pearl Zane Gray (the name he was born with, and didn't change until his twenties) was an outstanding pitcher. Some of his experiences as an amateur and semipro—such as being a "ringer" in a heated contest between two rural teams—are on display in these pages. The hero, Chase Alloway, takes his name from an Ohio professional whom Grey knew. Pearl's only equal on the local diamond was young brother Romer, or "Reddy," who went on to a notable career as a minor-league outfielder and even played one game in 1903 with the Pittsburgh Pirates. The redheaded

Romer, who is one of those mentioned in the dedication to *The Shortstop*, was later fictionalized as Reddy Ray in *The Young Pitcher* and in the story "The Redheaded Outfield."

When the Grey family moved to Columbus in 1890, the brothers joined the Capitols, a celebrated amateur club. The next year, a scout from the University of Pennsylvania saw Zane Grey defeat a strong Denison College team and offered him a scholarship. At Penn he came under the tutelage of Arthur "Sandy" Irwin, also mentioned in the dedication and fictionalized as Manager MacSandy in *The Shortstop* and, later, as Worry Arthurs in *The Young Pitcher*. Irwin was a star shortstop for several major-league teams and managed for eight years. Among many exploits during his four years of varsity ball, Grey (who shifted to the outfield in 1893, when the new pitching distance of sixty feet, six inches straightened his curveball) made a great catch at New York's Polo Grounds to help Penn defeat the New York Giants in a spring exhibition contest. In his senior year he hit a two-out, two-run homer in the ninth inning to vanquish the University of Virginia.

Grey also played professional ball for Wheeling in the Iron and Oil League of 1895 under a false name to maintain his college eligibility for 1896. Over the next four years he played in such minor leagues as the Interstate, the Atlantic, and the Eastern. Even after setting up his dentistry practice in New York City in 1899, Grey continued to play on weekends for the powerhouse Orange Athletic Club of Orange, New Jersey, a semipro outfit that played Sunday exhibitions against big-league clubs and frequently defeated them.

FOREWORD

Baseball in Zane Grey's time was very different from the game we know today. The mushy ball was "dead" and the fences were distant, so home runs were scarce; only a great slugger like Dan Brouthers could send the ball soaring as far as legions of lesser players later would. Runs had to be built one base at a time, so slap hitting and bunting were prime offensive tactics. Few pitchers could master the "drop," or modern curveball, which breaks vertically as well as laterally, so most of the curves thrown in this book are of the "roundhouse" or "schoolboy" variety, breaking only from side to side. The home team did not automatically bat last—it could choose the field or the bat, as it pleased. "Fixing"—colluding with gamblers to alter the outcome of the game—was appallingly common at all levels, including the majors. Playing baseball on the sabbath was a sacrilege in most American cities and towns, and "blue laws" regulating Sunday ball were enforced in big-league cities decades after the publication of Grey's book.

Ball players back then were heroes to boys and girls, but to most adults they were rowdies and loafers, uneducated and superstitious bumpkins, and certainly undesirable suitors for their daughters. Drunkenness was epidemic, as much a scourge then as drugs are today. Many drugs that are illegal today were over-the-counter drugstore purchases back then, and abuse of opium ("hittin' the pipe," as it is termed in these pages) was fairly common. The opportunity to hit an outfield sign and win a pair of shoes—available to players on the Findlay nine in *The Shortstop*—would be scorned by today's multimillionaires. Yet at the big-league level around 1910, batters took dedicated aim at the Bull Durham tobacco sign in each professional park in hopes of winning $50; and as late as the 1950s, batters on the Brooklyn Dodgers strove to hit the outfield sign of clothier Abe Stark, who rewarded them with a free suit.

Today, despite some continuing failures, our society affirms the basic human rights of the handicapped. One hundred years ago, however, disabled or malformed individuals were accorded little respect or dignity. Instead they were termed freaks, and magical traits were superstitiously ascribed to them that made them highly desirable as team mascots, like Mittie-Maru in *The Shortstop*. At the major-league level until about 1920, hunchbacks, dwarfs, and the mentally feeble were routinely hired as good-luck charms and sat in uniform on the bench or entertained the crowd before the game. (This view of the handicapped—or the merely "different," like left-handers—was hardly confined to baseball. Society at large feared the misshapen as manifestations of God's wrath, regarded the different as signs of God's humor, and attributed heightened goodness to the lame, like Tiny Tim in Charles Dickens's *A Christmas Carol*.)

If the baseball life was hard in 1890–1900, the period in which this novel takes place, that only mirrored the state of the nation. The western frontier was just closing, the Indian wars were just ending, and rural electrification was just beginning. The age of monopolies, trusts, and syndicates was in full flower, although almost everyone viewed them as evil (trust-busting on a big scale had commenced only a few years before Grey began this novel). Families headed by a mother and oldest son were appallingly common, created by poverty, alcohol abuse, or the death of a father. Children left school as early as the age of eight and often at the age of twelve, as Chase Alloway does here to help support his mother and crippled brother. College was a distant dream.

Boys deprived of boyhood grew up hard, often working in factories, becoming men with no sense of play. For such individuals, the spectator sport of baseball was a blessing, connecting them with the world from which they had been prematurely wrenched.

Women, blacks, Indians—none are treated with much dignity in this book, and in addressing *The Shortstop* to today's young reader, some offensive characterizations or phrasings have been refashioned. But much remains that the reader might question and compare with the notions prevalent today. Is Marjory Dean a lovely girl and a civilizing force on Chase Alloway? Or is she ("But I'm so stupid!") simply a ninny? Does Chase resolve the issue of Sunday baseball for himself in a responsible, clearheaded manner, or is he merely rationalizing what his heart tells him to do? Is he to be admired for standing up to a bully on the base paths, or is assaulting the bully with a horseshoe nail a tad excessive?

The joys of reading *The Shortstop* are in the small things: the bits of historical detail, the bygone expressions, the covert attitudes, and above all, the way that baseball mirrored and brightened life. As it still does.

JOHN THORN

PERSUADING MOTHER

CHASE ALLOWAY hurried out of the factory door and bent his steps homeward. He wore a thoughtful, anxious look, as of one who expected trouble. Yet there was a briskness in his stride that showed the excitement under which he labored was not altogether unpleasant.

In truth, he had done a strange and momentous thing; he had asked the foreman for higher wages, and being peremptorily refused, had quit his job, and was now on his way home to tell his mother.

He crossed the railroad tracks to make a short-cut, and threaded his way through a maze of smoke-blackened buildings, to come into a narrow street lined with frame houses. He entered a yard that could not boast of a fence, and approached a house as unprepossessing as its neighbors.

Chase hesitated on the steps, then opened the door. There was no one in the small, bare, clean kitchen. With a swing which had something of an air of finality about it, he threw his lunch box into a corner.

"There!" he said grimly, as if he had done with it. "Mother, where are you?"

Mrs. Alloway came in, a slight little woman, pale, with marks of care on her patient face. She greeted him with a smile, which faded quickly in surprise and dismay.

"You're home early, Chase," she said anxiously.

"Mother, I told you I was going to ask for more money. Well, I did. The foreman laughed at me and refused. So I quit my job."

"My boy! My boy!" faltered Mrs. Alloway.

Chase was the only breadwinner in their household of three. His brother, a bright, studious boy of fifteen, was a cripple. Mrs. Alloway helped all she could with her needle, but earned little enough. The winter had been a hard one and had left them with debts that must be paid. It was no wonder she gazed up at him in distressed silence.

"I've been sick of this job for a long time," went on Chase. "I've been doing a lot of thinking. There's no chance for me in the factory. I'm not quick enough to catch the hang of mechanics. Here I am over seventeen and big and strong, and I'm making six dollars a week. Think of it! Why, if I had a chance— See here, Mother, haven't I studied nights ever since I left school to go to work? I'm no dummy. I can make something of myself. I want to get into business—

business for myself, where I can buy and sell."

"My son, it takes money to go into business. Where on earth can you get any?"

"I'll make it," replied Chase eagerly. A flush reddened his cheek. He would have been handsome then, but for his one defect, a crooked eye. "I'll make it. I need money quick—and I've hit on the way to make it. I—"

"How?"

The short query drew him up sharply, chilling his enthusiasm. He paced the kitchen, and then, with a visible effort, turned to his mother.

"I am going to be a baseball player."

The horrible truth was out now and he felt relief. His mother sat down with a little gasp. He waited quietly for her refusal, her reproach, her arguments, ready to answer them one by one.

"I won't let you be a ballplayer."

"Mother, since Father left us to shift for ourselves I've been the head of the house. I never disobeyed you before, but now—I've thought it out. I've made my plan."

"Ballplayers are good-for-nothing loafers, rowdies. I won't have my son associate with them."

"They've a bad name, I'll admit; but, Mother, I don't think it's deserved. I'm not sure, but I believe they're not as black as they are painted. Anyway, even if they are, it won't hurt me. I've an idea that a young man can be honest and successful in baseball as in anything else. I'd rather take any other chance, but there isn't any."

"Oh! the disgrace of it! Your father would—"

"Now, see here, Mother, you're wrong. It's no disgrace. Why, it's a thousand times better than being a bartender, and I'd be that to help along. As for Father," his voice grew bitter, "if he'd been the right sort we wouldn't be here in this hovel. You'd have what you were once used to, and I'd be in school."

"You're not strong enough; you would get hurt," protested the mother.

"Why, I'm as strong as a horse. I'm not afraid of being hurt. Ever since last summer, when I made such a good record with the factory nine, this idea has been growing. They say I'm one of the fastest boys in Akron, and this summer the big nine at the roundhouse wants me. It's opened my eyes. With a little more experience I could get on a salaried team somewhere."

"You wouldn't go away?"

"I'll have to. And, Mother, I want to go at once."

Mrs. Alloway felt the ground slipping from under her. She opened her lips to make further remonstrance, but Chase kissed them shut, and, keeping his arm around her, led her into the sitting room. A pale youth, slight like his mother, sat reading by a window.

"Will," said Chase, "I've some news for you. Can you get through school, say in a year or less, and prepare for college?"

The younger boy looked up with a slight smile, such as he was wont to use in warding off Chase's persistent optimism. The smile said sadly that he knew he would never go to college. But something in Chase's straight eye startled him; then his mother's white, agitated face told him this was different. He rose and limped a couple of steps toward them, a warm color suddenly tingeing his cheeks.

"What do you mean?" he questioned.

Then Chase told him. In conclusion he said: "Will, there's big money in it. Three thousand a season is common, five for a great player. Who knows? Anyway, there's from fifty to a hundred a month even in these Ohio and Michigan teams, and that'll do to start with. You just take this from me: there'll be a comfortable home for Mother, you'll go to college, and later I'll get into business. It's all settled. What do you think of it?"

"It's great!" exclaimed Will, slamming down his book. There was a flame in his eyes.

Mrs. Alloway dropped her hands. She was persuaded. That from Will was the last straw. Tears began to fall.

"Mother, don't be unhappy," said Chase. "I am suited for something better than factory work. There's a big chance for me here. Mind you, I'm only seventeen. Suppose I play ball for a few years: I'll save my money, and when I'm twenty-two or twenty-five I can start a business of my own. It looks good to me!"

"But, my boy—if it—ruins you!"

"I don't like to see Chase leave us," said Will, "but I'm not afraid of that."

Mrs. Alloway dried her eyes, called up her smile, and told them she was not afraid of it either. Thereafter her composure did not leave her, though her sensitive lips quivered when she saw Chase packing a small grip.

"I don't want to take much," he mused, "and most of all I'll want my glove and ball shoes. Will, isn't it lucky about the shoes that college man gave me? They're full of spikes. I've never played in them, but I tried them on, and I'll bet I can run like a streak in them."

It was not long after that when he kissed his mother as she followed him to the doorway. Will limped after him a little way down the path and shook hands for the tenth time. His eyes were as wet as his mother's, but Chase's were bright and had a bold look.

"Chase, I never saw anyone who could run and throw like you, and I believe you'll make the greatest player in the whole country. Don't forget. It'll be hard at first. But you hang on! Hang on! There! Good luck! Good-bye!"

Chase turned at the corner of the street and waved to them. There was a lump in his throat which was difficult to swallow. But it was too late to go back, so he went forth bravely.

TWO

RIDING AWAY

THE fact that Chase had no objective point in mind did not detract from the new and absorbing charm of his situation. No more would he breathe the dust-laden air nor hear the din of the factory. He was free—free to go where he wished, to see new people and places, to find his fortune. He crushed back the pain in his throat; he reconciled himself to the parting from his mother and brother by the assurance that he could serve them best by doing so.

It was twilight when he reached the railroad tracks, where he stopped momentarily. Would he go to the left or to the right? A moment only did he tarry undecided; after all, there was only one course for him to start on and keep to, whether of direction or purpose, and that was to the right.

Darkness had settled down by the time he came to the outskirts of the town, and now secure in the belief that he would not be seen, he stopped to wait for a train. It was out of the question for him to think of riding in a passenger train. That cost money; and he must save what little he had. On Saturdays, before he left school, he had ridden on freight trains; and what he had done for fun he would now do in earnest. Some of the railroads running into town forbade riding, others did not care; and Chase took his stand by the track of one of the generous roads.

The electric lights shot up brightly, like popping stars out of the darkness, and a white glow arched itself over the town. Soon the shrill screech of a locomotive split the silence, then a rumbling and puffing told of an outward-bound freight. The gleam of a headlight streaked along the rails. Chase saw with satisfaction that the train was on his track, but he had an uneasy feeling that it was running too fast to be boarded. The huge black engine, like a one-eyed demon, roared by, shaking the earth. Chase watched the cars rattle by and tried to gauge their speed. It was so dark he could scarcely see, but he knew the train was running too fast to catch with safety. Still he did not hesitate. He waited a moment for an oil car, and as one came abreast he dashed with it down the track. Reaching up with his left hand, he grasped a handlebar. Instantly he was swung upward and slapped against the car. But Chase knew that swing, and it did not break his hold. As he dropped back to an upright position he felt for the footstep, found it, and was safe.

He climbed aboard and sat against the oil tank, placing his grip beside him. He laughed as he wiped the sweat from his brow. That was a time when the fun of boarding a freight did not appear. The blackness was all about him now, fields and woods and hills blurring by. The wind sang in his ears and cooled his face. The stars blinked above. The rasp and creak of the cars, the rhythmic click of the rails, the roar and rumble were music to him, for they sang of the passing miles between him and wherever he was going.

Lights of villages twinkled by like jack-o'-lanterns. These were succeeded after a while by the blank dim level of open country, which to Chase swept by monotonously for hours. Then a whistle enlivened him. He felt the engineer put on the air brake, then the bumping and jarring of cars and the grinding of wheels.

As the train slowed up Chase made ready to jump off. He did so presently, expecting to see the lights of a town, but there were none. He saw the shadow of a block-signal house against the dark sky, and concluded the engineer had stopped for orders at a junction crossing. Chase hurried along the tracks, found an open boxcar, and climbed in.

It was an empty car with a layer of hay on the floor. He groped his way in the gloom, found a corner, and lay down with his head on his grip.

It was warm and comfortable there; he felt tired, a drowsiness overcame the novelty of his situation, and he was falling asleep when he heard voices. Then followed the shuffling and scrambling noise made by several men climbing into the car. They went into another corner.

For a while he could not make out the meaning of their low, hoarse whispering; but as it grew louder he caught the drift. The men were thieves; they had robbed someone and were quarreling over the spoils. One of them had a thick, sullen voice, and it was evident that the other two were leagued against him.

The train started up with a rattle and clatter, gathered headway, and rolled on with a steady roar. From time to time Chase heard angry voices even above the din of the wheels. He was thankful for the dark and the noise. What they might do if they discovered him caused him to grow cold with fear. He shrank into the corner and listened. Whether it was after a few minutes or a long hour he had no idea, but when the whistle shrieked out again and the train slackened for another stop, he realized that the thieves were fighting. Hoarse cries and sodden blows, curses, and a deep groan told of a deed of violence.

"Let's beat it," whispered one, in the sudden silence. "Here comes a brakie."

The train had stopped. Footsteps grated out-

11

side, and streaks of light flickered into the car. Chase saw two men jump from the door and heard a brakeman accost them. He lay there trembling. What if the brakeman flashed his light into the car? What would be seen in the other corner? But the footsteps died away. Before he noticed it the train got in motion again; and he lay there wavering till the speed became so great that he dared not jump off.

To ride with a dead thief was not so frightful as to ride with a live one, thought Chase, but it was bad enough. His mind began to focus on one point, that he must get out of the car, and the more he thought the more fearful grew his state. While he lay there the train rolled on and the time flew by. All at once it appeared the blackness had given way to gray shadow. It grew lighter and lighter. He rose and went to the door. Day was dawning.

The train was approaching a hamlet, and ran parallel with a dusty road. Without a second's hesitation Chase leaped from the car. Through a rush of wind he alighted on his feet, bounced high, to fall heavily and roll over and over in the dust.

THREE

FAME

CHASE would have sustained worse bruises than he got to rid himself of the atmosphere of that car. When he was once free of it, however, he fell to wondering if the man were really killed. Perhaps he had only been wounded and was in need of assistance that Chase could have rendered. This thought cut him, but he dismissed it from mind, and addressed himself once more to his problem.

The village consisted of a few cottages; there was no railroad station, and on a siding stood a car marked "T. & O. C." Chase sat in the grass beside the track, and did not know whether to walk on or wait for another train. Meanwhile the sun rose warm and bright, shining on the bursting green leaves; meadowlarks sang in a field near by, and flocks of blackbirds winged irregular flight overhead. That May morning was full of life and hope for Chase, but even so, when two hours passed by with no train or even one person putting in an appearance, he began to grow restless and presently made a remarkable discovery. He was hungry. He had not given a thought to such a thing as eating. It was rather discomfiting to awaken to the fact that even in quest of fortune meals were necessary.

A column of blue smoke was curling lazily from one of the cottages, and thither Chase made his way. He knocked on the kitchen door, which was opened by a woman.

"Good morning," said Chase. "May I have a bite to eat?"

"You ain't a tramp?" queried she, eyeing him shrewdly.

"No, indeed. I can pay."

"I thought not. Tramps don't say 'Good mornin'.' I reckon you kin hev somethin'. Sit on the bench there."

She brought him milk, and bread and butter, and a generous slice of ham. While he was eating, a boy came out to gaze at him with round eyes, and later a lanky man with pointed beard walked up the path, his boots wet with dew.

"Mornin'," he said cheerily, "be yew travelin' fur?"

"Quite far, I guess," replied Chase. "How far is Columbus, or the first big place?"

"Wal, now, Columbus is a mighty long way, much as fifty miles, I calkilate. An' the nearest town to hum here is Jacktown, cross fields some five miles. It's a right pert place. It'll be lively today, by gum!"

"Why?" said Chase, with his mouth full of ham.

"Wal, Jacktown an' Brownsville hev it out today, an' I'll bet it'll be the doggonedest ballgame as ever was."

"Ballgame!"

"You bet. Jacktown ain't ever been beat, an' nuther has Brownsville. They've been some time gittin' together, but today's the day. An' I'll be there."

"I'm going, too," said Chase quietly. "I'm a ballplayer."

After Chase had crossed this Rubicon he felt more confident. He knew he would have to say it often, and he wanted practice. And the importance of his declaration was at once manifest in the demeanor of the man and the boy.

"Wal, I swan! You be, be you? I might hev knowed it, a strappin' young feller like you."

The boy's round eyes grew rounder and took on the solemn rapture of hero worship.

"How might I find my way to Jacktown?" inquired Chase.

"You might wait an' ride with me. Thet road leads over, round about. You can't miss it."

"Thank you, I shan't wait. I'll walk over. Good day." Chase headed into the grassy lane without knowing exactly why. The word "game" had attracted him, as well as the respective merits of the two teams; but it was mostly that he wanted to play. After consideration, it struck him that he would do well to get into a few games before he made application to a salaried team.

He spent the morning lounging along the green lane, sitting under a tree and on a mossy bank of a brook, and killing time in pretty places, so that when he reached Jacktown it was noon.

At the little tavern where he had lunch the air was charged with the electricity of a coming storm. The place was crowded with youths and men of homely aspect; all were wildly excited over the baseball game. He was regarded with an extraordinary amount of interest; and finally, when a tall individual asked him if he were a ballplayer, and he answered affirmatively, there was a general outburst.

"He's a ringer! Brownsville knowed they'd git beat with their hometeam, so they've loaded up!"

That was the burden of their refrain, and all Chase's stout denials in no wise mitigated their suspicion. He was a "ringer." To them he was an object of scorn and fear, for he had come from somewhere out of the vast unknown to wrest their laurels from them.

Outside little groups had congregated on corners and in the street, and suddenly, as by one impulse, they gathered in a crowd before the tavern. Ample reason there was for this, because some scout had sighted the approach of the visiting team. Chase gathered that Brownsville was an adjoining country town and, since time out of mind, a hated rival. Wagons and buggies, vehicles of all kinds and descriptions, filed by on the way to the ballgrounds; and a hay wagon with a single layer of hay and a full load of husky young men stopped before the tavern. The crowd inspected the load of young men with an anxiety most manifest, and soon remarks were heard testifying that the opposing team had grace enough to come with but one ringer.

The excitement, enthusiasm, and hubbub were amusing to Chase. He knew nothing of the importance of a game of ball between two country towns. While he was standing there a slim, clean-faced young man came up to him.

"My name's Hutchinson," he said. "I'm the schoolteacher over at Brownsville, and I'm here to catch the game for our fellows. Now, it appears there's some fuss about you being a ringer. We don't know you, and we don't care what Jacktown thinks. But the fact is, our pitcher hurt his arm and can't play. Either we play or forfeit the game. If you can pitch we'll be glad to have you. How about it?"

Chase assented readily, and moved to the hay wagon with Hutchinson, while the crowd hooted and yelled. Small boys kept up a running pace with the wagon and were not above flinging pebbles along with shouts of defiance. At the end of the village opened up a broad green meadow, upon which was the playground. There was a barn to one side, where the wagon emptied its load; and here the young men went within to put on their uniforms.

The uniform handed to Chase was the one belonging to the disabled pitcher, who must have been a worthy son of Ajax. For Chase was no stripling, yet he was lost in its reach and girth. The color of it stunned him. Brightest of bright red flannel, trimmed with white stripes, with white cotton stockings, this gorgeous suit voiced the rustic lads' enthusiasm for the great national game.

But when Chase went outside and saw the uniforms decorating the proud persons of the Jacktown nine he could hardly suppress a wild burst of mirth. For they wore blue caps, pink shirts, green trousers, and red stockings. Most of them were minus shoes, and judging from their activity were as well off without them. What was most striking to Chase, after the uniforms, was the deadly earnestness of the players of both teams. This attitude toward the game extended to the spectators crowding on the field. Chase did not need to be told that the whole of Jacktown was present and much of Brownsville.

Hutchinson came up to Chase then, tossed a ball to him, and said they had better have a little practice. After Chase had warmed up he began throwing the ball with greater speed and giving it a certain twist which made it curve. This was something he had recently learned. At first Hutchinson was plainly mystified; he could not get his hands on the ball. It would hit him on the fingers or wrists, and finally a swift in-shoot struck him in the stomach. Wherefore he came up to Chase and said:

"I never saw a ball jump like that. What do you do to it?"

"I'm throwing curves."

A light broke over the schoolmaster's face, and it was one of pleasure.

"I've read about it. You are throwing the new way. But these lads never heard of a curve. They'll break their backs trying to hit the ball. Now tell me how I shall know when you are going to throw a curve."

"You signal for what you want. When you kneel back of the batter, signal to me, one finger for a straight ball, two fingers for a curve."

"Good!" cried Hutchinson. After a little more practice he managed with the aid of his lately

19

acquired knowledge to get in front of Chase's curves and to stop them.

Presently a pompous individual wearing the Jacktown uniform came up to Chase and Hutchinson.

"Battin' order," he said, waving his pencil.

Hutchinson gave the names of his players, and when he mentioned Chase's the Jacktown man either misunderstood or was inclined to be facetious.

"Chaseaway? Is thet his name? Darn me, if he won't chase away to the tall timber."

He was the captain, and with a great show of authority called both teams to homeplate for the purpose of being admonished, lectured, and told how to play the game by the umpire. Chase had not seen this official, and when he did see him his jaw dropped. The umpire wore skin-tight velveteen knee trousers, black stockings, and low shoes with buckles. His striped shirt was arranged in a full blouse, and on the side of his head was stuck very wonderfully a small, jaunty cap. He addressed the players as if he were the arbiter of fate, and he lifted his voice so that the audience could receive the benefit of his eloquence and understand perfectly the irrevocable nature of the decisions he was about to render. In conclusion, he recited a number of baseball rules in general and ground rules in particular, most remarkable in themselves and most glaringly designed to favor the hometeam. Chase extracted from the complexity of one of these rules that on a passed ball behind the catcher, or an overthrow at first, when Jacktown was at bat the player could have all the bases he could make; and when Browns- ville was at bat, for some inscrutable reason, this same rule did not hold.

Then this master of ceremonies ordered the Jacktown team into the field, tripped like a ballet dancer to his position behind the catcher, and sang out in a veritable clarion blast: "P–l–a–a–y b–a–w–l!"

Chase could scarcely remove his gaze from the umpire, but as his turn to bat came in the first inning he directed his attention to the Jacktown pitcher. He remembered that someone had said this important member of the Jacktowns was the village blacksmith. After one glance, Chase did not doubt it. The pitcher was a man of enormous build, and his bared right arm looked like a branch of a rugged oak tree. The first ball he shot toward the homeplate resembled a thin white streak.

"O–n–e s–t–r–i–i–k–e!" shrieked the umpire.

Two more balls similar to the first retired the batter, and three more performed the same ser- vice for the second batter. It was Chase's turn next. He was a natural hitter and had perfect confidence. But as the first ball zipped past him, looking about the size of a pea, he knew he had never before faced such terrific speed. Nor did he have the power to see in that farmer blacksmith one of the greatest pitchers the game was ever to produce. Chase struck at the next two balls and was called out. Then the Jacktown players trooped in, to the wild clamor of their supporters.

When Chase saw some of the big Jacktown fellows swing their bats he knew he would have an easy time with them, for they stood with their feet wide apart, and held their bats with the left hand over the right, which made a clean, straight swing impossible. He struck out the first three batters on nine pitched balls.

For several innings it went on in that manner, each club blanking the other. When Brownsville came in for their fifth inning at bat, Chase got Hutchinson to call all the players around him in a bunch.

"Boys," he said, "we can hit this Jacktown pitcher. He throws a straight ball, almost always waist-high. Now, you all swing too hard. Let's choke the bat—hold it halfway up instead of by the handle—and poke at the ball. Just meet it."

The first player up, acting on Chase's advice, placed a stinging hit into right field. Whereupon the Brownsville contingent on the sidelines rose in a body and roared their appreciation of this feat. The second batter hit a groundball at the

shortstop, who fielded it perfectly, but threw wild
to the first baseman. And the third hitter sent up
a very high fly. The whole Jacktown team made
a rush to try to catch the ball when it came down.
It went so high that it took some time to drop,
all of which time the Brownsville runners were
going like mad around the bases. When the ball
returned to earth, so many hands were raised to
clutch it that it bounced away to the ground. One
runner had scored, and two were left, on second
and third bases respectively.

Chase walked to the plate with determination.
He allowed the first ball to go by, but watched it
closely, gauging its speed and height. The next
one he met squarely with a solid crack. It shot
out over second base, went up and up, far beyond
the fielder. Amid the delirious joy of the Brownsville partisans the two runners scored ahead of
Chase, and before the ball could be found he too
reached home.

The Jacktown players went to pieces after that
and fumbled so outrageously and threw so errat-
ically that Brownsville scored three more runs
before the inning was over.

Plain it was that when Jacktown came in for
their turn at bat nothing short of murder was
impossible for them. They were wild-eyed and
hopped along the baselines like Indians on the
warpath. But yell and rage and strive all they

knew how, it made no difference. They simply could not get their bats to connect with Chase's curves. They did not know what was wrong. Chase delivered a slow, easy ball that apparently came sailing like a balloon straight for the plate, and just as the batter swung his bat the ball suddenly swerved so that he hit nothing but the air. Some of them spun around, so viciously did they swing, but not one of them so much as touched the ball. The giant pitcher grunted like an ox when he made his bat whistle through the air; and every time he swung at one of the slow, tantalizing balls to miss it, he frothed at the mouth in his fury. His reputation as a great hitter was undone that day and he died hard.

In the eighth inning, with the score 11 to 0, matters were serious when the Jacktown team came in for their turn at bat. They whispered mysteriously and argued aloud, and acted altogether like persons possessed. When the first batter faced Chase the other players crowded behind the plate, where already a good part of the audience was standing.

"It's his eye, his crooked eye," said one player, pointing an angry finger. "See thet! You watch him, an' you think he's goin' to pitch the ball one way, an' it comes another. It's his crooked eye, I tell you!"

A sympathetic murmur from the other players

and the crowd attested to the value of this re-markable statement. The first batter struck fu-tilely at the balls, which were getting slower and more exasperating, and when he had missed three he slammed his bat on the ground and actually jumped up and down in his anger. The second batter aimed at a slow-coming ball and swung with all his might, only to hit a hole in the air.

With that the umpire tripped lightly before the plate, and standing on his tiptoes, waved his hand to the spectators. His eyes were staring with ex-citement, and on his cheek blazed the hue of righteous indignation.

"Ga-me cal-led!" he yelled in his penetrating tenor. *"Game called, 9 to 0, favor Jacktown!* BROWNSVILLE PITCHER THROWS A CROOKED BALL!"

Pandemonium broke loose among the specta-tors. They massed on the field in inextricable con-fusion. The noise was deafening. Hats were in the air, and coats, and everything else available for throwing.

Hutchinson fought his way through the crazy crowd and, grasping Chase, pulled him with no gentle hand from the mob in the direction of the barn. Once out of the tumult he said:

"Hurry and change. I don't like the looks of things. These Jacktown fellows are rough. I think we'd better hurry out of town."

It was all so amusing to Chase that he could not help laughing, but soon Hutchinson's sober aspect, and the wild anger of the other Brownsville players, who poured noisily into the barn, put a different coloring on the affair. What had been pure fun for him was plainly a life-and-death matter to these rustics. They divided their expression in mauling Chase with fervid congratulations and declarations of love, and passionate denunciations of the umpire and the whole Jacktown outfit.

Suddenly, as loud shouts sounded outside the barn, Hutchinson ran out, to return at once with a startled look.

"You've got to run for it!" he cried. "They're after you; they're in a devil of a temper. They'll ride you on a fencerail, or tar-and-feather you. Hurry! You can't reason with them now. Run for it. You can't wait to dress."

One look down the field was sufficient for Chase. The Jacktown players were marching toward the barn. The blacksmith led the way, and over his shoulder hung a long fencerail. Behind them the crowd came yelling.

"Run for it!" cried Hutchinson, greatly excited. "I'll fetch your clothes."

Chase had removed all his uniform except stockings and shoes, and he had put on his shirt. Grabbing up his hat, trousers, and coat, he bounded out of the door and broke down the field like a scared deer.

When the crowd saw him they let out a roar that lent wings to his feet. It frightened him so that he dropped his trousers, and did not dare stop to recover them. Over his shoulder he saw the Jacktown players, with the huge pitcher in the lead, start after him.

The race was close only for a few moments. Chase possessed a fleetness of foot that now served him in good stead and undoubtedly had never appeared to such advantage.

With his hair flying in the wind, with his shirt-tails standing straight out behind him, he sped down the field, drawing so rapidly away that his pursuers seemed not to be running at all.

FOUR

VICISSITUDE

NOT until he had leaped fences and crossed half a dozen fields did Chase venture to look back. When he did so, he saw with immense relief that he had outdistanced his pursuers. Several were straggling along in front of the others, but all stopped running presently, sending after him a last threatening shout.

It made Chase as angry as a wet hornet. With all the power of his lungs he yelled back at them: "Hayseeds! Hayseeds!" Then at the sight of his bare knees he took to laughing till he nearly cried. What would his brother Will have thought of that run? What would his mother have thought? This last sobered him instantly. Whenever he remembered her, the spirit of adventure fled, leaving him with only the uncertainty of his situation.

"It won't do to think of Mother," he soliloquized, "for then I'll lose my nerve. Now what'll I do if those dunderheaded hayseeds steal my pants? I'll be in a bad fix."

He climbed a knoll which stood about a mile

from the ballgrounds and from which he could
see the surrounding country. The sun slowly sank
in the west. Chase watched and watched and
strained his eyes, but he could not see anyone
coming. The sun went down, leaving a red glow
behind the hills; twilight, like a gray shadow,
seemed to steal toward him from the fields.

He had noted a haystack at the foot of the knoll,
and after one more hopeless glance over the dark-
ening meadows, he went down to it. He had visited farms in the country often enough to know
that haystacks left to the cattle usually had caves
in them; and he found this one with a deep cavern,
dry, sheltered, and sweetly odorous of musty hay.

"If things keep up the way they've started for
me I'm likely to find worse beds than this," he
muttered.

He discovered he was very tired, and that the
soft hay was conducive to a gradual relaxing of his
muscles. But his mind whirled round and round.
Would Hutchinson come? What had happened to
the other Brownsville players? A savage bunch,
that Jacktown nine! How easy it had been to fool
them with a simple, slow roundhouse curve!

"It's his crooked eye! He looks one way an'
pitches another!" That jaunty umpire with his
dainty shoes and velvet knickerbockers—wherever on earth did he come from?

So Chase played the game over in his mind,

once more ran his desperate race, to come back to his predicament and the fear that he might not recover his trousers. At length sleep put an end to his worry.

In the night he awoke, and seeing a bright star, which only accentuated the darkness, smelling the fragrant hay, and hearing a strange sound, he did not realize where he was, and a chill terror crept over him. This soon passed. Still the low sound bothered him. Stretching forth his hand, he encountered a furry coat and heaving warm body. A cow had sought the shelter of the haystack and lay beside him chewing her cud.

"Hello, Bossy!" said Chase. "I'd certainly rather sleep with a nice, gentle cow like you than with a dead old thief."

The strangeness of it all kept him awake for a while. The night was very quiet, the silence being unbroken save for the *"Peep, peep"* of spring frogs and the low munching beside him. He asked himself if he were afraid, and said, "No," but was not sure. Things seemed different in the dark and loneliness of night. Then his brother's words— "Hang on!"—rang out of the silence, and, repeating these in his heart, he stored up strength for the future, and once more fell asleep.

The sun was rosy red on the horizon when he awakened. His gentle friend stood browsing on the grass near at hand, and by way of beginning the day well he said, "Good morning," to her.

"Now what to do!" he said seriously. "There's no use to expect anyone now, and no use to go back to look for my trousers."

The problem seemed unsolvable, when he saw a farmer in the field, evidently come out to drive up the cows. Chase covered his nakedness as well as possible with his coat and hailed him. The farmer came up, slapped his knee with a big hand, and guffawed.

"Gol' darn my buttons, if it ain't thet Chaseaway feller! Say, I was over there yestiddy an' seen the whole show. Best thing I ever seen, b'gosh! I'm a Brownsville boy, I am. Now you come along with me. I'll git a pair of overalls fer you an' a bite to eat. But you must light out quicker'n you'd say 'Jack Robinson,' fer two of my farmhands played yestiddy, an' they're hoppin' mad."

The kindhearted farmer hid Chase in a woodshed near his house and presently brought him a pair of overalls and some breakfast. Chase right gladly covered his chilly legs. Once more he felt his spirits rise. Fortunately his pocketbook had been in his coat, so it was not lost. When he offered to pay the farmer, that worthy refused to accept any money, and said he and everybody who was ever born in Brownsville were everlastingly bound to be grateful to a lad called Chaseaway.

Then, under direction from the farmer, Chase started cross-country with the intention of finding the railroad and making for Columbus. When he reached the railroad he had to take the spikes off his baseball shoes, for they hurt his feet. He started westward along the track. Freight trains passed him, going too fast for him to board, so he walked all day. Nightfall found him at a village, where after waiting an hour he caught a west-bound freight and reached Columbus at ten o'clock. He stumbled around over the tracks in the yards, climbed over trains, and made his way into the city. He secured a room in a cheap lodging house and went to bed.

In the morning he got up bright and early, had breakfast, and bought a copy of the Ohio *State Journal.* He knew Columbus had a baseball team in the Tri-State League, and he wanted to read the news. The very first column he saw on the baseball page contained, in flaring headlines, the words:

"CHASEAWAY, THE CROOKED-EYE WONDER, HOODOOS THE GREAT JACKTOWN NINE!"

He could not believe his eyes. But the words were there, and they must have reference to him. With feverish haste he read the detailed account that followed the headlines. He gathered that the game had been telephoned to the baseball editor of the *Journal,* who, entirely overlooking Jacktown's tragical point of view, had written the game up in a spirit of fun. He had written it so well, and had drawn such a vivid picture of the Jacktown players, and especially of his own "Chase-away" with his shirttails flying, that Chase laughed despite his mortification and chagrin.

He gloomily tore out the notice, put it in his pocket, and started off to put Columbus far behind him. The allusion to his crooked eye hurt his feelings, and he resolved never to pitch another game of ball. There were other positions he could play better.

It was Chase's destiny to learn that wherever he went his fame had preceded him.

In Black Lick he was told he might get a rail ride there; at Newark the wise boy fans recognized him at once and hooted him off the ground before he could see the manager of the team; the Mansfield captain yelled for him to take himself and his hoodoo off into the woods; Galion players laughed in his face; Upper Sandusky wags advised him to go back to scaring cows in the cornfields.

Every small town in Ohio, as well as every large one, supported a baseball club, and Chase dragged himself and the hoodoo that haunted him from place to place. The Niles team played him in right field one day, and, losing the game, promptly set him adrift. He got a chance on the Warren nine and here again his hoodoo worked.

Lima had a weak aggregation and readily gave him an opportunity to make good. He was nervous and overstrained, and made five errors, losing the game.

He drifted to Toledo, to Cleveland, thence back to Toledo and over into Michigan. It seemed that fortune favored him with opportunities that he could not grasp. Adrian, Jackson, Lansing, Owosso, Flint—all the clubs that took him on for a game lost it, and further spread the fame of his hoodoo.

Chase's money had long since departed from him. His clothes became ragged and unclean. Small boys called him "Hobo," and indeed in all except heart he was that. For he rode on coal trains and cattle trains, and begged his few and scanty meals at the back doors of farmhouses.

In every town he came to he would search out the baseball grounds, waylay the manager or captain, say that he was a player and ask for a chance. Toward the end of this time of vicissitude no one had interest enough in him to admit him to the grounds.

Back he worked into Ohio, growing more weary, more downhearted, till black despair fixed on his heart. One morning he awoke stiff and sore in a fence corner outside of a town. He asked a woman who gave him bread to eat what the name of the town was, and she said Findlay.

Chase thought bitterly of how useless it would be to approach the manager of that team, for Findlay was in the league, and moreover, had been for two years the crack team of Ohio. He did not even have any intention of trying. There was nothing left for him but to go back home and beg to be taken into the factory at his old job and poor wages. They did not seem so bad now, after all his experience. Alas for his dreams!

It occurred to him in wonder that he had persisted for a long time in the face of adverse circumstances. It was now June, though he did not know the date, and he had started out in May. Why had he kept on? For weeks he had not thought of his mother and brother, and now, quite suddenly, they both flashed into his mind. Then he knew why he had persisted, and he knew more—that he would never give up.

He saw her smile, and the warm light of faith in Will's eyes, and he heard his last words: "Hang on, Chase. Hang on!"

THE CRACK TEAM OF OHIO

In the afternoon of that day Chase was one of the forerunners of the crowd making towards the Findlay ballpark.

Most ballparks were situated in the outskirts of towns; Findlay, however, being a red-hot baseball center, had its grounds right in town on a prominent street. They were enclosed with a high board fence, above which the roof of a fine grandstand was to be seen. Before the gates the irrepressible small boy was much in evidence.

As Chase came up he saw a ball fly over the stand, fall to the street, and bound away, with the small boys in a wild scramble after it. To secure the ball meant admission to the grounds. Quick as a flash Chase saw his opportunity and dashed across the street. He got the ball, to the infinite disgust of the small boys. The gatekeeper took it and passed Chase in.

Players in gray uniforms marked "Kenton" were practicing, some out in the field, others on the diamond. Chase had never seen such a smooth baseball ground. The diamond was bare; all the rest of the field was green, level sward, closely cropped. Chase thought a fellow who could not play well there was not worth much. As the noisy crowd poured in, filling the bleachers, and more slowly the grandstand, he thrilled to think what it would mean to him to play there.

Then when the thought came of what little chance he had, the old heartsickness weighed him down again. By and by he would ask to see the manager, but for the moment he wanted to put off the inevitable.

He stood in the aisle between the grandstand and bleachers, leaning over the fence to watch the players. A loud voice attracted him. He turned to see a very large, florid man, wearing a big diamond, addressing a small man whose suit of clothes was as loud as the other fellow's voice.

"Hey, Mac, what's the matter with this bunch of dead ones you've got? Eleven straight games lost! You're now in third place, and dropping fast, after starting out to set the pace. Findlay won't stand for it."

The little man bit savagely at the cigar, tilting it up in line with his stub nose; and the way he frowned lowered the brim of his hat.

"Sure, it's a slump, Mr. Beekman," he said, in conciliatory tones. "Now, you know the game; you're up; you're up on the fine points. You ain't like most of them wooden-headed directors. The boys ain't been hittin'. Castorious is my only pitcher whose arm ain't gone lame this cold spell. I've been weak at shortstop all this spring. But we'll come around, now you just take that from me, Mr. Beekman."

The pompous director growled something and went on up to the grandstand steps. Then a very tall fellow with wide, sloping shoulders and red hair accosted the little man.

"Say, Mac, what was he beefing about? I heard him speak my name. Did he have his hammer out?"

"Hello, Cas. No, Beekman ain't knockin' you. He was knockin' me. Sore on me, because we're losin'."

"If some of those stiffs would stay away from the grounds and stop telling us how to play the game we'd sooner break our bad streak. Are you going to work me today?"

"How's your arm?"

"Good. It's getting strong. What I need is work. When I get my speed I'll make these puff-hitters lay down their bats."

With that, Castorious swaggered into the dressing room under the grandstand, followed by the little manager.

Chase left his post, went to the door, hesitated when he saw the place full of ballplayers in various stages of dressing, and then entered and walked straight up to the manager.

"I heard you say you needed a shortstop. Will you give me a chance?"

He spoke distinctly, so that everyone in the room heard him. The manager looked up to speak when Castorious bawled out:

"Fellows, here he is! He's been camping on our trail. I said somebody had Jonahed us. It's the crooked-eye hoodoo!"

Ballplayers are superstitious, and are like sheep inasmuch as that they follow one another. The uproar that succeeded upon Castorious's discovery showed two characteristic traits—the unfailing propensity of the players to make game of anyone, and the real anxiety with which they regarded any of the signs or omens traditionally disastrous.

How well they recognized Chase showed the manner in which they followed anything written about baseball.

"Hello, there, Chaseaway!"

"Where's your pants?"

"Hoodoo!"

"Jonah!"

"Don't look at me with that eye."

"To the woods for yours!"

Chase stood there bravely, with the red mantling his face, waiting for the manager to speak. Once or twice Mac attempted to make himself heard and, failing, turned on his gibing players and ordered them to shut up. Then he said:

"Are you really the fellow they're making fun of?"

"Yes."

"But he was a pitcher. You said you could play short."

"I can play anywhere."

"Let me see your mitts; stick out your hands."

Chase's hands were broad, heavy, with long, powerful fingers.

"You're pretty young, ain't you? Where have you played?"

Chase told his age and briefly outlined his late experience.

"Name 'Hoodoo' followed you, eh? Been up against it hard?"

"Yes."

Mac laughed and said he knew how that was, then thoughtfully pulled on his cigar. Now it chanced that he was not only an astute manager, but a born trainer of ballplayers as well. He never overlooked an opportunity. He had seen seedier-looking fellows than Chase develop into stars that set the baseball world afire. Nevertheless, having played the game himself, he was not exempt from its little peculiarities and superstitions. If his team had been winning he certainly would have thrown any slant-eyed applicant out of the grounds.

His small, shrewd eyes studied Chase intently.

"I'll play you at short today. Barnes, get this fellow a suit."

Barnes, the grounds keeper, opened a locker and threw a uniform on the floor at Chase's feet. His surly action was significant of how thoroughly he had assimilated his baseball education. But he did not say anything nor did the players, for at that moment there was a stern decisiveness about the little manager which brooked no interference. Ordinarily Mac was the easiest-going fellow in the world, overrun and ruled by his players; sometimes, however, he showed an iron hand. But when he had left the dressing room a storm burst over poor Chase's head.

"You blank-eyed idiot! What do you want to jinx the team for?"

"This is a championship club, Sonny."

"Don't look at me with your bum lamp!"

"I want my notice. I'm through with Findlay."

"Now for the toboggan! Last place for ours!"

Used as Chase had become to the manner of badinage directed at him, he had never encountered it like this. The players spoke good-naturedly, and a laugh followed each particular sally; nevertheless they were in deadly earnest and seemed to consider his advent a calamity which he could have spared them. He dressed in silence and avoided looking at them, as if indeed their conviction was becoming truth to him, and went out on the grounds.

He got through the few moments of practice

creditably, but when the gong rang, calling the players in for the game to begin, a sudden nervousness and nausea made him weak, blind, trembling. The crowded grandstand blurred indistinctly in his sight. The players moved in a sort of haze, and what he heard sounded far off.

Chase started into that game with a nightmare. When at the bat he scarcely saw the ball and was utterly at the mercy of the Kenton pitcher. In the field he wobbled when the ball came toward him; it bounded at him like a rabbit; it was illusive and teasing, and seemed to lure him to where it was not; it popped out of his hands, and slipped like oil between his legs; it had a fiendish propensity for his shins, and though it struck sharply it seemed to leave no pain. On the solitary occasion when he did get his hands squarely on the ball he threw it far over the first baseman's head, far over the right field bleachers.

He was dimly conscious that the game was a rout; that the Findlay players, rattled by his presence, sore at his misplays, went to pieces and let Kenton make a farce out of it. He heard the growls of disapproval from the grandstand, the roar from the bleachers, the hooting and tin-canning from the small boys.

And when the game ended he sneaked off the field, glad it was all over, and entered the dressing room in a sick and settled hopelessness.

Roar on roar greeted him. He fell on a bench and bowed his head in his hands. The scorn, invective, anger, and caustic wit broke about his deadened ears.

Presently Castorious stalked into the room followed by Mac and several directors of the club. Cas was frothing at the mouth; big brown freckles shone through his pale skin; his jaw was set like a bulldog's.

With the demeanor of a haughty chieftain approaching a captive bound to the stake, he went up to Chase and tapped him on the shoulder.

"Say! did anybody, *did* anybody, DID anybody ever tell you you could play ball?"

Chase lifted his face from his hands and looked at Cas.

"Yes," he said, with a wan smile, "but I guess they were mistaken."

Cas opened his lips to say something further, but the words never came. He took a long look at Chase, then went to his locker, sat down, and with serious, thoughtful brow began changing his clothes.

Mac's sharp voice suddenly stilled the babel in the room.

"Gentlemen, either I run this team my own way or not at all. That's it. I'm ready to resign now."

"Here, here, Mac, cool down!" said one.

"We're perfectly satisfied with you. We know we couldn't fill your place. Beekman was a little hasty. He's a hard loser, you know. So never mind what's been said. Pull the team out of this rut— that's all we want. We've got confidence in you, and whatever you say goes. If you want money to get a new player or two to strengthen up, why speak out. Findlay must be in front."

"Gentlemen, I don't need any money; I'm carryin' sixteen players now, an' I've got the best team in this league. All I want is a little luck."

"Well, here's hoping you get it." The directors shook hands with Mac and filed out of the dressing room.

When they were out of hearing the little manager turned to his players. He seemed to expand, to grow tall; his face went white, his small eyes snapped.

"Morris, go to the office an' get your money," he said. "Stanhope, you've got ten days' notice. Ziegler, the bench for yours without pay till you can hold your tongue. Now, if any of the rest of you fellows have some ideas about runnin' this team, sing 'em out!"

He stamped up and down the room before them, waiting with blazing eyes for their replies, but none came.

"Cas!" he shouted, confronting that individual. "Are you a liar?"

"Wha-at?" demanded Cas, throwing his head forward like a striking hawk.

"Are you a liar?"

"No, I'm not. Who says so? I'll take a punch—"

"Did you try to pitch today?"

"I had no steam; couldn't break a pane of glass," replied Cas evasively.

"Stow that talk. Did you try?"

"No, I didn't," said Cas sullenly.

"Now, ain't that a fine thing for you to do? You, the best pitcher in this league, with more'n one big manager watchin' your work! Ain't you ashamed of yourself?"

Cas did not say so, but he looked it.

"I've got somethin' to say to the rest of you muckers. Of all the rotten quitters you are the worst I ever seen. That exhibition you gave today would have made a dead one out of a five-thousand-volt storage battery. Here you are, a bunch of stickers that the likes of ain't in the rest of the league—and you fall down before a measly little slowball, a floater that babies could hit! You put the boots on every grounder in sight! You let flyballs bounce off your head! You pegged the ball in the air or at somebody's shins! It just takes a bad spell of luck to show some fellows' yellow

45

streaks. Saffron ain't nothin' to the color of some of you."

As Mac paused for breath someone grumbled, "Hoodooed!"

"Bah! You make me sick," cried Mac. "Suppose we've been hoodooed? Suppose we've fallen into a losin' streak? It's time to bust somethin', ain't it?"

Then his manner altered, his voice became soft and persuasive.

"Boys, we've got to break our slump. Now, there's Cas—you all know what a great twirler he is. An' he throwed us down. Look at the outfield. Where's one outside of the big leagues thet can rank with mine? An' they played today with two wooden legs. Look at Benny an' Meade—why, to-day they were tied to posts. Look at reliable old Hicks behind the plate—today he missed third strikes, overthrew the bases, an' had eight passed balls. An' say, did any of you steady up this youngster who I was givin' a chance? Did any of you remember when you was makin' your first bid for fast company? Now, I ain't got no more to say to you, except we're goin' to brace an' we're goin' through this league like sand through a sieve!"

With that he turned to Chase, who had listened and now was ready to get his summary dismissal.

"Didn't make nothin' of the chance you asked for, did you?" he said brusquely.

Chase shook his head.

"Lost your nerve at the critical time, when you had a chance to make good. Here I need a shortstop who is fast, an' can hit an' throw; an' you come along trailin' a hoodoo an' muss up the game. Put my team on the bum!"

Then there was a silence, in which Mac walked to and fro before Chase, who still sat with head bowed.

"Now you see what losin' your nerve means. You're fast as lightnin' on your feet, you've got a great arm, an' you stand up like a hitter. But you lost your nerve. A ballplayer mustn't never lose his nerve. See what a chance you had? I'm weak at short. Now, after I turn you down you won't never get such a chance again."

He kept pacing slowly before Chase, watching him narrowly; and when Chase at last lifted his pale, somber face from his hands, Mac came to a sudden stop. With some deliberation he put his hand into his coat pocket and brought forth a book and papers. Then in a different voice, in the same soft tones with which he had ended his talk to the other players, he said to Chase:

"Here's twenty-five dollars advance, an' your contract. It's made out, so all you need to do is sign it. A hundred per month for yours! Don't stare at me like thet. Take your contract. You're on! An' as sure as my name's MacSandy I'll make a star of you!"

47

FIRST INNINGS

WHEN Chase left the grounds his eyesight was still as blurred as it had been during the game, only now from a different source. His misery fell from him like a discarded cloak. He kept his hand deep in his right trouser pocket, clutching the twenty-five dollars as if it were the only solid substance to give actuality to this dream of bliss. First he thought he would send all the money to his mother; then he reflected that as he resembled the most ragged species of tramp he must spend something for at least respectable clothing.

He entered a secondhand store, where he purchased for the sum of five dollars a complete outfit, even down to shoes and hat. It was not much on style, Chase thought, but clean and without a rip or hole. With this precious bundle under his arm he set out to find the address given him by Mac, where he could obtain board and lodging at a reasonable rate. After some inquiry he found the street and eventually the house, which, because of a much more pretentious appearance than he had supposed it would have, made him hesitate.

But following a blindly grateful resolve to do anything and everything that Mac had told him, he knocked on the door. It opened at once to show a stout matron of kindly aspect, who started somewhat as she saw him.

Chase said he had been sent there by Mac, and told his errand, whereupon the woman looked relieved.

"Exkoose me," she replied, "come righdt in. I haf one rooms, a putty nice one, four thalers a weeg."

She showed Chase a large room with four windows, a big white bed, a table and bureau, and chairs and a lounge; and with some difficulty managed to convey to him that he might have it and board for the sum of four dollars weekly. When he was certain she had not made a mistake he lost no time in paying her for a week in advance. Good fortune was still such a stranger to him that he wanted to ensure himself against moments of doubt.

He washed and dressed himself with a pleasure that had not been his for many a day. Quite diligently did he apply the comb and brush Mrs. Obenwasser had so kindly procured. His hair was long and a mass of tangles, and it was full of cinders, which reminded him grimly of his dearly earned proficiency as a nightrider on fast mail trains and slow freights.

"That's all over, thank Heaven!" breathed Chase. "I hope I can forget it." But he knew he never would.

When he backed away from the mirror and surveyed his clean face and neat suit, and saw therein a new Chase, the last vanishing gleam of his doubt and unhappiness left him. The supper bell, ringing at that moment, seemed to have a music of hope; and he went downstairs hungry and happy. Several young men at the table made themselves agreeable to him, introduced themselves as clerks employed downtown, and incidentally dyed-in-the-wool baseball fans. Chase gathered that Mrs. Obenwasser was a widow of some means and kept boarders more out of the goodness of her heart and pride in her table than from any real necessity. Chase ate like a famished wolf. Never had meat and biscuits and milk and pie been so good. And it was shame that made him finally desist, not satisfied appetite.

After supper he got paper, pen, and ink from his landlady and went to his room to write home. It came to him with a sudden shock that he had never written since he left. What could they have thought? But he hastened to write, for he had good news. He told Will everything, though he skimmed over it lightly, as if his vicissitudes were but incidents in the rise of a ballplayer. He wrote to his mother, telling her of his good fortune, of the promise of the future, of his good health and spirits. Then he enclosed all his money, except a dollar or so in silver, in the letter and sealed it. Try as hard as he might, Chase could not prevent his tears from falling on that letter, and they were sealed up with it.

Then he sallied forth to look for the post office and incidentally to see something of Findlay. He was surprised to find it a larger and more prosperous place than he had supposed. Main Street was broad and had many handsome buildings. The avenues leading from it were macadamized and lined with maple trees. Chase strolled round a block and saw many fine brick residences and substantial frame houses with vine-covered, roomy porches and large lawns. Back on Main Street again he walked along without aim. There was a hotel on the next corner, and a number of young men were sitting outside with chairs tilted back against the window, and also on the edge of the sidewalk. Chase had sauntered into the ken of his fellow players.

"Say, fellers, will you get onto thet!"

"It's Chaseaway!"

"Hello, Chase, old sport, come an' have a drink."

"Dude Thatcher, we can see your finish. Our

51

new shortstop is some on the dress himself. He'll show you up!"

"Would you mind droppin' your lid over thet lame blinker? I won't want to have the willies tonight."

Then an incident diverted their attack on Chase. Someone kicked a leg of Enoch Winters's chair, and being already tipped far back, it over-balanced and let Enoch sprawl in the gutter. Whereupon the group howled in glee.

"Cap'n, wasser masser?" enquired Benny, trying to help Enoch to his feet and falling over him instead. Benny was drunk. Slowly Enoch sep-arated himself from Benny and righted his chair and seated himself.

"Now, ain't it funny?" said he.

His slow, easy manner of speaking, without a trace of resentment, made Chase look at him. Enoch was captain of the team and a man long past his boyhood. Yet there remained something boyish about him. He had a round face and a round bullet head, cropped close; round gray eyes, wise as an owl's; and he had a round lump on his right cheek. As this lump moved up and down, Chase presently divined that it was only a puffed-out cheek over a quid of tobacco. He in-stinctively liked his captain, and when asked to sit down in a vacant chair near at hand he did so, with the pleasant thought that at last he was one of them.

Chase sat there for over an hour, intensely interested in all of them, in what they said and did. He felt sorry for Benny, for the second baseman was much under the influence of liquor, had a haggard face and unkempt appearance. The fellow called Dude Thatcher was a tall youth, good-looking, very quiet, and very well dressed. Chase saw him flick dust off his shiny shoes and more than once adjust his spotless cuffs. Meade was a typical ballplayer, under twenty, a rugged and bronzed fellow of jovial aspect. Hicks would never see thirty again; there was gray hair over his temples; he was robust of build and his hands resembled eagles' claws. He was a catcher, and many a jammed and broken finger had been his lot.

What surprised Chase more than anything was the fact that baseball was not once mentioned by this group. They were extremely voluble, too, and talked on every subject under the sun except the one that concerned their occupation. Under every remark lay a subtle inflection of humor. Mild sarcasm and sharp retort and ready wit flashed back and forth.

The left fielder of the team, Frank Havil by name, a tall, thin fellow with a pale, sanctimonious face, strolled out of the hotel lobby and seated himself near Chase. And with his arrival came a series of most peculiar happenings to Chase. At first he thought mosquitoes or flies were bothering him; then he imagined a wasp or hornet was butting into his ear; next he made sure of one thing only: that something was hitting the side of his face and head. Whatever it was he had no idea. It came at regular intervals and began to sting more and more. He took a sidelong glance at Havil, but that young man's calm, serious face disarmed any suspicion. But when Havil got up and moved away the strange fact that the stinging sensation ceased to come caused Chase to associate it somehow with the quiet left fielder.

"Chase, did you feel anythin' queer when Havil was sittin' alongside of you?" asked Winters.

"I certainly did. What was it?"

"Havil is a queer duck. He goes round with his mouth full of number ten shot, an' he works one out on the end of his tongue, an' flips it off his front teeth. Why, the blame fool can knock your eye out. I've seen him make old bald-headed men crazy by sittin' behind them an' shootin' shot onto the bald spots. An' he never cracks a smile. He can look anybody in the eye, an' they can't tell he's doin' it, but they can feel it blamed well. He sure is a queer duck, an'—you look out for your one good eye."

"Thank you, I will. But I have two good eyes.

I can see very well out—out of the twisted one."

Chase went to his room and to bed. Sleep did not come soon. His mind was too full; too much had happened; the bed was too soft. He dozed off, to start suddenly up with the bump of a freight train in his ears. But when he did get to sleep it was in a deep, dreamless slumber that lasted until ten o'clock the next morning. After breakfast, which Mrs. Obenwasser had kept waiting for him, he walked out to the ballgrounds to find the gates locked. So with morning practice out of the question he returned to Main Street and walked toward the hotel.

He saw Castorious sitting in the lobby.

"Hello, Chase, now wouldn't this jar you?" he said in friendly tones, offering a copy of the Findlay *Chronicle*.

Could this be the talking monster that had roared at him yesterday, and scared about the last bit of courage out of him? Cas laid a big freckled hand on the newspaper and pointed out a column.

BASEBALL NOTES

"Mac gave Morris his walking papers yesterday and Stanhope his notice. This is a good move, as these players caused dissension in the club. Now we can look for the brace. Findlay has been laying down lately. Castorious's work yesterday is an example. We would advise him not to play that dodge anymore.

"The new shortstop, Chaseaway, put the
boots on everything that came his way, but for
all that we like his style. He is fast as lightning
and has a grand whip. He stands up like Brouthers, and if we're any judge of ballplayers—here
we want to say we've always called the turn—
this new youngster will put the kibosh on a few
and 'chase' the Dude for batting honors."

Chase read it over twice and it brought the hot
blood to his face. After that miserable showing of
his in the game—how kind of the reporter to
speak well of him! Chase's heart swelled. He had
been wrong—there were lots of good fellows in
the world.

"Make a fellow sick, wouldn't it?" said Cas, in
disgust. "Accused me of laying down! Say, come
and walk over to the hotel where the Kenton
fellows are staying."

Chase felt very proud to be seen with the great
pitcher, for whom all passersby had a nod or a
word. They stopped at another hotel, in the lobby
of which lounged a dozen broad-shouldered, red-
faced young men.

"Say," said Cas, with a swing of his head, "I
just dropped in to tell you guys that I'm going to
pitch today, and I'm going to let you down with
two hits. See!"

A variety of answers were flung at him, but he
made no reply and walked out. All the way up

the street Chase heard him growling to himself.

The afternoon could not come soon enough for Chase. He went out to the grounds in high spirits. When he entered the dressing room he encountered the same derisive clamor that had characterized the players' manner toward him the day before. And it stunned him. He looked at them aghast. Every one of them, except Cas, had a scowl and hard word for him. Benny, not quite sober yet, was brutal, and Meade made himself particularly offensive. Even Winters, who had been so friendly the night before, now said he would put out Chase's other lamp if he played poorly today. They were totally different from what they had been off the field. A frenzy of some kind possessed them. Roars of laughter following attacks on him, and for that matter on each other, detracted little, in Chase's mind, from the impression of unnatural sarcasm.

He hurriedly put on his uniform and got out of the room. He did not want to lose his nerve again. Cas sat on the end of the bleachers, pounding the boards with his bat.

"Say, I was waiting for you," he said in a whisper to Chase. "I'm going to put you wise when I get a chance to talk. All I want to say now is, I'll show up this Kenton outfit today. They can't hit my speed, and they always hit my slowball to left field, through short. Now you lay for them. Play deep and get the ball away quick. You've got the arm for it."

This was Cas's way of showing his friendship, and it surprised Chase as much as it pleased him. Mac came along then, and at once said:

"Howdy, boys. Cas, what are you dressed for?"

"I want to work today."

"You do? What for?"

"Well, I'm sore about yesterday, and I'm sore on—Kenton, and if you'll work me today I'll shut them out."

"You're on, Cas, you're on," said Mac, rubbing his hands in delight. "Thet's the way I want to hear you talk. We'll break our losin' streak today."

Then Mac pulled Chase aside, out of earshot of the players pouring from the dressing room, and said,

"Lad, are you goin' to take coachin'?"

"I'll try to do everything you tell me," replied Chase.

"Sure, thet's good. Listen, I'm goin' to teach you the game. Don't ever lose your nerve again. Got thet?"

"Yes."

"When you're in the field with a runner on any base make up your mind before the ball's hit what to do with it if it should happen to come to you. Got thet?"

"Yes."

"Play a deep short unless you're called in. Come in fast on slow-hit balls; use an underhand snap throw to second or first base when you haven't lots of time. Got thet?"

"Yes."

"When the ball is hit or thrown to any baseman, run with it to back up the player. Got thet?"

"Yes."

"All right. So far so good. Now as to hittin'. I like the way you stand up. You're a natural-born hitter, so stand your own way. Don't budge an inch for the speediest pitcher as ever threw a ball. Learn to dodge wild pitches. Wait, watch the ball. Let him pitch. Don't be anxious. Always take a strike if you're first up. Try to draw a base on balls. If there's runners on the bases look for a sign from me on the bench. If you see my score-card stickin' anywhere in sight, hit the first ball pitched. If you don't see it—wait. Turn around, easy like, you know, an' take a glance my way after every pitched ball, an' when you get the sign—hit. We play the hit-an'-run game. If you're on first or any base, look for the same sign from me. Then you'll know what the batter is up to an' you'll be ready. Hit an' run. Got thet?"

"Yes, I think so."

"Well, don't get rattled even if you do make a

mistake, an' never, never mind errors. Go after everythin' an' dig it out of the dust if you can, but never mind errors!"

"An' Chase, wait," called Mac, as the eager youngster made for the field. Then in a whisper, as if he were half afraid some of the other players would hear, he went on: "Don't sass the umpire. Don't ever speak to no umpire. If you get a rotten deal on strikes, slam your bat down, puff up, look mad, do anythin' to make a bluff, but don't sass the umpire. See!"

"I never will," declared Chase.

The Findlay team came on the grounds showing the effects of the shake-up. They were an aggressive, stormy aggregation. Epithets the farthest remove from complimentary flew thick and fast as the passing balls. A spirit of rivalry pervaded every action. In batting practice he who failed to send out a clean hard hit received a volley of abuse. In fielding practice he who fumbled a ball or threw too high or too low was scornfully told to go out on the lots and play with the kids. It was a merciless warfare, every player for himself, no quarter asked or given.

Chase fielded everything that came his way and threw perfectly to the bases, but even so, the players, especially Meade, vented their peculiar spleen on him as well as on others who made misplays. All of which did not affect Chase in the least. He was on his mettle; his blood was up. The faith Mac had shown in him should be justified, that he vowed with all the intensity of feeling of which he was capable.

The gong sounded for the game to start, and Castorious held forth in this wise:

"Fellows, I've got everything today. Speed—well say! it's come back. And my floater—why, you can count the stitches! You stiffs get in the game. If you're not a lot of cigar-store Indians, there won't be anything to it."

Big and awkward as Cas was in citizen dress, in baseball harness he made an admirable figure. The crowds in the stands had heard of his threat to the Kentons—for of all gossip, that in baseball circles flies the swiftest—and were out in force and loud in enthusiasm. The bleachers idolized him.

As the players went for their positions Cas whispered a parting word to Chase: "When you see my floater go up, get on your toes!"

The umpire called play, threw out a white ball, and stood in an expectant posture.

As Cas faced the first Kenton player he said in low voice: "Look out for your noggin!" Then he doubled up like a contortionist and undoubled to finish his motion with an easy, graceful swing. With wonderful swiftness the white ball traveled straight for the batter's head. Down he fell flat,

jumped up with red face, and yelled at Cas. The
big pitcher smiled derisively, received the ball
from the catcher, and with the same violent effort
delivered another ball, but with not half the speed
of the first. The batter had instinctively stepped
back. The umpire called the ball a strike.

" 'Fraid to stand up, hey?" enquired Cas, in
the same low, tantalizing voice.

When he got the ball again he faced the batter,
slowly lifted his long left leg, and seemed to turn
with a prodigious step toward third base, at the
same instant delivering the ball to the plate. The
ball evidently wanted to do anything but reach
its destination. Slowly it sailed, soared, floated,
for it was one of Cas's floaters.

The batter half swung his bat, pulled it back,
then poked at the ball helplessly. The result was
an easy grounder to Chase, who threw the runner
out.

It was soon manifest to Chase that Cas worked
differently from any pitcher he had ever seen.
Instead of trying to strike out any batters, Cas
made them hit the ball. He never threw the same
kind of a ball twice. He seemed to have a hundred
different ways for the ball to go. But always he
vented his scorn on his opponents in the low sarcasm which may have been heard by the umpire,
but was inaudible to the audience.

At the commencement of the third inning nei-

ther side had yet scored. It was Chase's first time
up, and as he bent over the bats trying to pick
out a suitable one, Cas said to him:

"Say, Kid, this guy'll be easy for you. Wait him
out now. Let his curveball go."

Chase felt perfectly cool when he went up. The
crowd gave him a great hand, which surprised but
did not disconcert him. He stood square up to
the plate, his left foot a little in advance. He
watched the Kenton pitcher with keen eyes; he
watched the motion, and he watched the ball as
it sped toward him rather high and close to his
face. He watched another, a wide curve, go by.
The next was a strike, the next a ball, and then
following, another strike. Chase had not moved
a muscle. The bleachers yelled: "Good eye, old
man! hit her out now!"

With the count three-and-two Chase lay back
and hit the next one squarely. It rang off the bat,
a beautiful liner that struck the right field fence
a few feet from the top. Chase reached third base,
overran it, to be flung back by Cas. The crowd
roared.

Winters, the captain, came running out and
sent Cas to the bench. Then he began to coach.

"Look out, Chase! Hold your base on an infield
hit! Play it safe! Play it safe! Here's where we make
a run, here's where we make a run! Here's where
we make a run! Hey, there, pitcher, you're up in

the air already! Oh! What we won't do to you!
Steady, Chase, now you're off. Hit it out, old man!
That's the eye! Make it good! Mugg's Landing!
Irish stew! Lace curtains! Ras-pa-tas! Oh my—"

Bawling at the top of his voice, spitting tobacco
juice everywhere, with wild eyes and sweaty face,
Winters hopped up and down the coaching line.
When Benny put up a little fly back of second
Winters started Chase for the plate and ran with
him. The ball dropped safe and the run scored
easily.   When Chase went panting to the bench
Mac screwed up his stubby cigar and gazed at his
new find with enraptured eyes. "I guess maybe
thet hit didn't bust our losin' streak!"

Whatever Chase's triple had to do with it, the
fact was that the Findlay players suddenly recovered their batting form. For two weeks they
had been hitting atrociously, as Mac said, and now
every player seemed to find hits in his bat.
Thatcher tore off three singles; Cas got two and
a double; and the others hit in proportion.

Chase rapped another against the right field
fence, hitting a painted advertisement that gave
a pair of shoes to every player performing the
feat; and to the delirious joy of the bleachers and
stands, at his last time up, he put the ball over
the fence for a home run.

It was a happy custom of the oilmen of Findlay,
who devoted themselves to the game, to throw

64

silver dollars out of the stands at the player making a home run. A bright shower of this kind completely bewildered Chase. He picked up ten, and Cas handed him seven more that had rolled in the dust.

"A suit of clothes goes with that hit, me boy," sang out Cas.

It was plainly a day for Chase and Cas. The Kenton players were at the mercy of the growling pitcher. When they did connect with the ball, sharp fielding prevented safe hits. Chase had eleven chances, some difficult, one particularly being a hard bounder over second base, all of which he fielded perfectly. But on two occasions fast, tricky baserunners deceived him, bewildered him, so that instead of throwing the ball he held it. These plays gave Kenton the two lonely runs chalked up to their credit against seventeen for Findlay.

"Well, we'll give you those tallies," said Cas, swaggering off the field. He had more than kept his threat, for Kenton made but one safe hit.

"Wheeling tomorrow, boys," he yelled in the dressing room. "We'll take three straight. Say! Did any of you cheapskates see my friend Chase hit today? *Did* you see him? Oh! I guess he didn't put the wood on a few! I guess not! Over the fence and far away! That one is going yet!"

Chase was dumbfounded to hear every player

speak to him in glowing terms. He thought they had bitterly resented his arrival, and they had; yet here was each one warmly praising his work. And in the next breath they were fighting among themselves. Truly these young men were puzzles to Chase. He gave up trying to understand them.

A loud uproar caused him to turn. The players were holding their sides with laughter, and Cas was doing a Highland fling in the middle of the floor. Mac looked rather white and sick. This struck Chase as remarkable after the decisive victory, and he asked the nearest player what was wrong.

"Oh! nuthin' much! Mac only swallowed his cigar stub!"

It was true, as could be plainly seen from Mac's expression. When the noise subsided he said:

"Sure, I did. Was it any wonder? Seein' this dead bunch come back to life was enough to make me swallow my umbrella. Boys," here a smile lighted up his smug face, "now we've got thet hole plugged at short the pennant is ours. We've got 'em skinned to a frazzle!"

SEVEN

MITTIE-MARU

"CHASE, you hung bells on 'em yestiddy."

Among the many greetings Chase received
from the youngsters swarming out to the grounds
to see their heroes whip Wheeling, this one struck
him as the most original and amusing. It was given
him by Mittie-Maru, the diminutive hunchback
who had constituted himself as mascot of the
team. Chase had heard of the boy and had seen
him on the day before but not to take any particular notice.

"Let me carry yer bat."

Chase looked down upon a sad and strange little
figure. Mittie-Maru did not much exceed a yard
in height; he was all misshapen and twisted, with
a large head which was set deep into the hump
on his shoulders. He was only a boy, yet he had
an almost useless body and the face of an old man.

Chase hurriedly lifted his gaze, thinking with
a pang of self-reproach how trifling was his
crooked eye compared to the hideous deformity
of this lad.

"Three straight from Wheelin' is all we want," went on Mittie-Maru. "We'll skin the coal diggers all right, all right. An' we'll be out in front trailin' a merry 'Ha! Ha!' fer Columbus. They're leadin' now, an' of all the swelled bunches I ever seen! Put it to us fer three straight when they was here last. But we got a bad start. Then I got sick an' couldn't report, an' somehow the team can't win without me. Yestiddy was my first day fer—I don't know how long—since Columbus trimmed us."

"What was the matter with you?" asked Chase.

"Aw! nuthin'. Jest didn't feel good," replied the boy. "But I got out yestiddy, an' see what you done to Kenton! Say, Chase, you takes mighty long steps. It ain't much wonder you can cover ground."

Chase modified his pace to suit that of his companion, and he wanted to take the bat, but Mittie-Maru carried it with such pride and conscious superiority over the envious small boys who trooped along with them that Chase could not bring himself to ask for it.

As they entered the grounds and approached the door of the clubhouse Mac came out. He wore a troubled look.

"Howdy, Mittie; howdy, Chase," he said in a loud voice. Then as he hurried by he whispered close to Chase's ear, "Look out for yourself!"

This surprised Chase so that he hesitated. Mittie-Maru reached the dressing room first and, turning to Chase, he said, "Somethin' doin', all right, all right!"

This was soon manifest, for as Chase crossed the threshold a chorus of yells met him.

"Here he is—now say it to his face!"

"Salver!"

"Jollier!"

"You mushy soft-soaper!"

Then terms of opprobrium fell about his ears so thickly that he could scarcely distinguish them. And he certainly could not understand why they were being made. He went to his locker, opened it, took out his uniform, and began to undress. Mittie-Maru came and sat beside him. Chase looked about him to see Winters lacing up his shoes and taking no part in the vilification. Benny was drunk. Meade's flushed face and thick speech showed that he, too, had been drinking. Even Havil made a sneering remark in Chase's direction. Chase made note of the fact that Thatcher, Cas, and Speer, one of the pitchers, were not present.

"You're a Molly!" yelled Meade. "Been makin' up to the reporters, haven't you? Fixin' it all right for yourself, eh? Playin' for the newspapers? Well, you'll last about a week with Findlay."

"What do you mean?" demanded Chase.

"Go wan!" shouted the first baseman. "As if you hadn't seen the *Chronicle!*"

"I haven't," said Chase.

"Flash it on him," cried Meade.

Someone threw a newspaper at Chase, and upon opening it to the baseball page he discovered his name in large letters. And he read an account of yesterday's game, which, excepting to mention Cas's fine pitching, made it seem that Chase had played the whole game himself. It was extravagant praise. Chase felt himself grow warm under it, and then guilty at the absence of mention of other players who were worthy of credit.

"I don't deserve all that," said he to Meade, "and I don't know how it came to be there."

"You've been salvin' the reporter, jollyin' him."

"No, I haven't."

"You're a liar!"

A hot flame leaped to life inside Chase. He had never been called that name. Quickly he sprang up, feeling the blood in his face. Then as he looked at Meade, he remembered the fellow's condition, and what he owed to Mac, and others far away, with the quieting effect that he sat down without a word.

A moment later Benny swaggered up to him and shook a fist in his face.

"I'm a-goin' t' take a bing at yer one skylight an' shut it fer ye."

Chase easily evaded the blow and arose to his feet.

"Benny, you're drunk."

Matters might have become serious then, for Chase, undecided for the moment what to do, would not have overlooked a blow, but the gong ringing for practice put an end to the trouble. The players filed out.

Mittie-Maru plucked at Chase's trousers and whispered,

"You ought to 've handed 'em one!"

Chase's work that afternoon was characterized by the same snap and dash which had won him the applause of the audience in the Kenton games. And he capped it with two timely hits that had much to do with Findlay's victory. But three times during the game, to his consternation, Mac took him to task about certain plays. Chase ran hard back of second and knocked down a basehit, but he could not recover in time to throw the runner out. It was a splendid play, for which the stands gave him thundering applause. Nevertheless, as he came in to the bench Mac severely reprimanded him for not getting his man.

"You've got to move faster 'n thet," said the little manager testily. "You're slow as an ice wagon."

And after the game Mac came into the dressing room, where Chase received a good share of his displeasure.

71

"Didn't you say you knew the game? Well, you're very much on the blink today. Now the next time you hit up a flyball, don't look to see where it's goin', but run! Keep on runnin'. Fielders muff flies occasionally, an' someday runnin' one out will win a game. An' when you make a basehit, don't keep on runnin' out to the foul flag just because it's a single. Always turn for second base, an' take advantage of any little chance to get there. If you make any more dumb plays like thet they'll cost you five each. Got thet?"

Chase was mystified, and in no happy frame of mind when he left the grounds. Evidently what the crowd thought good playing was quite removed from the manager's consideration of such.

"Hol' on, Chase," called Mittie-Maru from behind.

Chase turned to see the little mascot trying to catch up with him. It suddenly dawned on Chase that the popular idol of the players had taken a fancy to him.

"Say, Cas tol' me to tell you to come to his room at the hotel after supper."

"I wonder what he wants. Did he say?"

"No. But it's to put you wise, all right, all right. Cas is a good feller. Me an' him has been friends. I heard him say to Mac not to roast you the way he did. An' I wants to put you wise to somethin' myself. Mac's stuck on you. He can't keep a smile

off his face when you walk up to the plate, an'
when you cut loose to peg one acrost he just stut-
ters. Oh! he's stuck on you, all right, all right!
'Boys, will you look at thet swing?' he keeps sayin'.
An' when you come in he says you're rotten to
yer face. Don't mind Mac's roasts."

All of which bewildered Chase only the more.
Mittie-Maru chattered about baseball and the
players, but he was extremely reticent in regard
to himself. This latter fact, in conjunction with
his shabby appearance, made Chase think that all
was not so well with the lad as it might have
been. He found himself returning Mittie-Maru's
regard.

"Good-bye," said Mittie-Maru at a cross street.
"I go down here. See you tomorrer."

After supper Chase went to the hotel, and
seeing that Cas was not among the players in the
lobby, he found his room number, and with no
little curiosity mounted the stairs.

"Come in," said Cas in answer to his knock.

The big pitcher sat in his shirtsleeves blowing
rings of smoke out of the open window.

"Hello, Chase; was waiting for you. Have a
cigar. Don't smoke? Throw yourself around comfortable—but say, lock the door first. I don't want
anyone butting in."

Chase found considerable relief and pleasure
in the friendly manner of Findlay's star pitcher.

"I want to have a talk with you, Chase. First, you won't mind a couple of questions."

"Not at all. Fire away."

"You're in dead earnest about this baseball business?"

"I should say I am."

"You are dead set on making it a success?"

"I've got to." Chase told Cas briefly what depended on his efforts.

"I thought as much. Well, you'll find more than one fellow trying the same. Baseball is full of fellows taking care of mothers and fathers and orphans, too. People who pay to see the game and keep us fellows going don't know just how much good they are doing. Well, Chase, it takes more than speed, a good eye, and a good arm and head to make success."

"How so?"

"It's learning how to get along with managers and players. I've been in the game ten years. Most every player who has been through the mill will let the youngster find out for himself, let him sink or swim. Even managers will not tell you everything. It's baseball ethics. I'm overstepping it because—well, because I want to. I don't mind saying that you're the most promising youngster I ever saw. Mac is crazy about you. All the same, you won't last two weeks on the Findlay team, or a season in fast company, unless you change."

"Change? How?"

"Now, Chase, don't get sore. You're a little too soft for this business. You're too nice. Lots of boys are that way, but they don't keep so and stay in baseball. Do you understand me?"

"No, I don't."

"Well, baseball is a funny game. It's like nothing else. You've noticed how different the players are off the field. They'll treat you right away from the grounds, but once in uniform, look out! When a professional puts on his uniform he puts on his armor. And it's got to be bulletproof and spike-proof. The players on your own team will get after you, abuse you, roast you, blame you for everything, make you miserable, and finally put you off the team. This may seem to you a mean thing. But it's the way of the game. When a new player is signed everybody gets after him, and if he makes a hit with the crowd, and particularly with the newspapers, the players get after him all the harder. In a way, that's a kind of professional jealousy. But the main point I want to make clear to you is the aggressive spirit of the players who hold their own. On the field ball playing is a fight all the time. It's good-natured and it's bitter-earnest. Every man for himself! Survival of the fittest! Dog eat dog!"

"Then I must talk back, strike back, fight back?"

"Exactly. Else you will never succeed in this

business. Now, don't take a bad view of it. Baseball is all right; so are the players. The best thing is that the game is square—absolutely square. Once on the inside, you'll find it peculiar, and you've got to adapt yourself."

"Tell me what to do."

"You must show your teeth, my boy, that's all. The team is after your scalp. Apart from this peculiarity of the players to be eternally after someone, I'm sure they like you. Winters said you'd make a star if you had any sand. Thatcher said if you lasted you'd make his batting average look sick. One of them, I think, has it in for you just because he's that sort of a guy. But I mention no names. I'm not a knocker, and let me tell you this—never knock any lad in the business. The thing for you to do, the sooner the better, is to walk into the dressing room and take a punch at somebody. And then declare yourself strong. Say you'll punch the block off anyone who opens his trap to you again."

"And after that?"

"You'll find it different. They'll all respect you; you'll get on better for it. Then you'll be one of us. Play hard, learn the game, keep sober—and return word for word, name for name, blow for blow. After a little this chewing the rag becomes no more to you than the putting on of your uniform. It's part of the game. It keeps the life and ginger in you."

"All right. If I must—I must," replied Chase, and as he spoke the set of his jaw boded ill to someone.

"Good. I knew you had the right stuff in you. Now, one thing more. Look out for the players on the other teams. They'll spike you, knee you, put you out, if they can. Don't ever slide to a base headfirst, as you did today. Some second baseman will jump up and come down on you with both feet, and break something, or cut you all up. Don't let any player think you are afraid of him, either."

"I'm much obliged to you, Cas. What you've told me explains a lot. I suppose every business has something about it a fellow don't like. I'll do the best I can, and hope I'll make good, as Mittie-Maru says."

"There's a kid with nerve!" exclaimed Cas enthusiastically. "Best fan I ever knew. He knows the game, too. Poor little beggar!"

"Tell me about him," said Chase.

"I don't know much. He turned up here last season, and cottoned to the team at once. Someone found out that he ran off from a poorhouse, or home for incurables or bad boys or something. There was a fellow here from Columbus looking for Mittie, but never found him. He has no home, and I don't know where he lives. I'll bet it's in a garret somewhere. He sells papers and shines shoes. And he's as proud as he's game—you can't give him anything. Baseball he's crazy over."

"So is my brother, and he's a cripple too."

"Every boy likes baseball, and if he doesn't, he's not a boy."

Chase left Castorious then and went downstairs, for he expected to meet several of the young men who boarded with him, and who had invited him to spend the evening with them. They came presently and carried him off to an entertainment in one of the halls. Here his new friends, Harris, Drake, and Mandle, led him from one group of boys and girls to another, and introduced him with evident pride in their opportunity. It was a church fair and well attended. Chase had never seen so many pretty girls. Being rather backward, he did not very soon notice what was patent to all—that he was the young man of the hour—and when he did see it he felt as if he wanted to run away. Facing Mac and the players was easier than trying to talk to these gracious ladies and whispering, arch-eyed girls. Ice cream was the order of the evening, and as long as Chase could eat he managed to conceal his poverty of speech; but when he absolutely could not swallow another spoonful he made certain to get away.

When four girls in white vivaciously appropriated him and whirled him off somewhere, his confusion knew no bounds. His young men friends basely deserted him and went to different parts of the hall. He was lost, and he gave up. From booth to booth they paraded with him, all chattering at once. He became vaguely aware that he was spending money and attaching to himself various articles; he caught himself saying he would like very much to have this and that, which he did not want at all.

The evening passed very quickly and like a dream. Chase found himself out of the bright lights in the cool darkness of the night. He walked two blocks past his corner. He reached his room at length, struck a light, and saw that he had an armful of small bundles and papers. He made the startling discovery that he had purchased four lace-fringed pincushions, a number of handpainted doilies, one sewing basket, one apron, two match-scratchers, one gorgeous necktie, and one other article that he could not name.

Discomfited as he was, Chase had to laugh. It was too utterly ridiculous. Then more soberly he began to count the money he had, in order to find out what he had spent. The sum total of his rash expenditures amounted to a little over five dollars.

"Five dollars!" ejaculated Chase. "For this stuff

and about a gallon of ice cream. That's how I save my money. Confound those girls!"

But Chase did not mean that about the girls. He knew the evening had been the pleasantest one he could remember. He tried to recollect the names of the girls and how they looked. This was impossible. Nothing of that wonderful night stood out clearly: as a whole, it left a confused impression of music and laughter, bright eyes and golden hair, smiles and white dresses.

Next morning he wrote to his mother and told her all about it, adding that she must not take the expenditure of his money so much as an instance of reckless extravagance as it was a case of highway robbery.

In the afternoon on the way to the ballpark he met Mittie-Maru and, relating last night's adventure, asked him if he could use a pincushion or two.

"Not on yer life!" cried Mittie-Maru. "Sorry I didn't put you wise to them church sociables. They tricked you, Chase. Sold you a lot of duds. You want to stay shy of thet bunch, all right, all right."

"Don't you ever go to church?"

"I went to Sunday school last fall. Miss Marjory, she was in the school, got me to come. She's a peach. Sweeter 'n a basket of red monkeys. She was all right, all right, but I couldn't stand the

preacher, an' some others, so I quit. An' every
time I see Miss Marjory I dodge or hit it up out
of sight."

"What was wrong with the preacher?"

"He's young, an' I think preachers oughter be
old. He fusses the wimmen folks too hard. He
speaks soft an' prays to beat the band, an' everybody thinks he's an angel. But—oh, I ain't a
knocker."

"Wait for me after the game?"

"Sure. An' say, Chase, are you goin' to stand
fer the things Meade calls you?"

"I'm afraid I can't stand it much longer."

If anything, Chase's reception in the dressing
room was more violent than it had been the day
before. Nevertheless he dressed without exchang-
ing a word with anyone. This time, however, he
was keenly alert to all that was said and to who
said it. All sense of personal affront or injustice,
such as had pained him yesterday, was now ab-
sent. He felt himself immeasurably older; he
coolly weighed this harangue at him with the stern
necessity of his success, and found it nothing.

And when he went out upon the field he was
conscious of a difference in his feelings. The mist
that had bothered him did not now come to his
eyes; nor did the contraction bind his throat; nor
did the nameless uncertainty and dread oppress
his breast. He felt a rigidity of muscle, a deadli-

ness of determination, a sharp, cold confidence. The joy of playing the game, as he had played it ever since he was big enough to throw a ball, had gone. It was not fun, not play before him, but work—work that called for strength, courage, endurance.

Chase gritted his teeth when the umpire called: "Play ball!" and he gritted them throughout the game. He staked himself and all he hoped to do for those he loved, against his own team, the opposing team, and the baseball world. He saw his one chance, a fighting chance, and he meant to fight.

When the ball got into action he ran all over the field like a flash. He was everywhere. He anticipated every hit near him, and scooped up the ball and shot it from him, with the speed of a bullet. He threw with a straight, powerful overhand motion and the ball sailed low, with terrific swiftness, and held its speed. He grabbed up a hit that caromed off Winters's leg, and though far back of third base, threw the runner out with time to spare. He caught a foul fly against the left field bleachers. He threw two runners out at the plate, and that from deep short.

He beat out an infield hit; he got a clean single into right field; and for the third time in three days he sent out a liner that by fast running he stretched into a three-bagger. Findlay had clinched the game before this hit, which sent in two runners, but for all that, the stands and bleachers rose as a body and cheered. The day before Chase had doffed his cap in appreciation of their applause. Today he did not look at them. He put the audience out of his mind.

But with all his effort, speed, and good luck he made an unfortunate play. It came at the close of the eighth inning. Wheeling got runners on second and third, with only one out. The next man hit a sharp bouncer to Chase. He fielded the ball, and expecting the runner on third to dash for home he made ready to throw him out. But this runner held his base. Chase turned to try to get the batter going down to first, when the runner on second ran right before him toward third. Chase closed in behind him, and as the fellow slowed up tried to catch him. Then the runner on third bolted for home. Chase saw him and threw to head him off, but was too late.

In the dressing room after the game the players howled about this one run that Chase's stupidity had given Wheeling. They called him "wooden-head," "sap-head," "sponge-head," "dead-head." Then Mac came in and delivered himself.

"Put the ball in your pocket! Put the ball in your pocket, didn't you? Countin' your money, wasn't you? Thinkin' about the girls you was with last night, hey? Thet play costs you five. See! Got thet? You're fined. After this when you get the ball an' some runner is hittin' up the dust, throw it. Got thet? Throw the ball! Don't keep it! Throw it!"

When the players' shout of delight died away, Chase turned on the little manager.

"What d'you want for fifteen cents—canary birds?" he yelled, in a voice that rattled the windows. He flung his bat down with a crash, and as it skipped along the bench more than one player fell over himself to get out of its way. "Didn't I say I had to learn the game? Didn't you say you'd show me? I never had that play before. I didn't know what to do with the ball. What d'you want, I say? Didn't I accept nine chances today?"

Mac looked dumbfounded. This young lamb of his had suddenly roused into a lion.

"Sure you needn't holler about it. I was only tellin' you."

Then he strode out amid a silence that showed the surprise of his players. Winters recovered first, and turned his round red face and began to bob and shake with laughter.

"What—did he—want for fifteen cents—canary birds? Haw! Haw! Haw!"

In another moment the other players were roaring with him.

EIGHT

ALONG THE RIVER

CASTORIOUS blanked the Wheeling club the next day, and the following day Speer won his game. Findlay players had returned to their old form and were getting into a fast stride, so the *Chronicle* said. Three straight from Columbus, was the slogan! Mac had signed a new pitcher, a left-hander named Poke, from a nearby country village, and was going to develop him. He was also trying out a popular player from the high school team.

Mac had ordered morning practice for the Columbus series of games. The players hated morning practice—"drill" they called it—and presented themselves with visible displeasure. And when they were all on the grounds Mac appeared with a bat over his shoulder and with his two new players in tow.

Poke was long and lanky, a sun-burned rustic who did not know what to do with his hands and feet.

"Battin' practice," called out Mac, sharply, ordering Poke to the pitcher's box.

Poke peeled off his sweater, showing bare arms that must have had a long and intimate acquaintance with ax and woodpile.

"Better warm up first," said Mac.

"It developed that Poke did not need any warmup. When he got ready he wound himself up, and going through some remarkable twist that made him resemble a cartwheel, delivered the ball toward the plate. Thatcher just dodged in time to save his head.

"Speed! Whew! Wow!" exclaimed the players.

"Speed!" echoed Thatcher. "Wait till you get up there!"

Poke drove Thatcher away from the plate and struck Meade out.

"Put 'em over!" said Benny as he came up.

The first ball delivered hit Benny on the foot and, roaring, he threw down his bat.

"You Rube! You wild Indian! I'll git you fer thet!"

Enoch Winters was the next batter.

"Say, you lean, hungry-lookin' rubberneck, if you hit me—" warned Enoch in his soft voice.

Poke struck Enoch out and retired Chase on a little popup. Then Cas sauntered up with his wagon-tongue bat and a black scowl on his face.

"Steady up, steady up," said he. "Put 'em over. Don't use all your steam."

"Mister, I ain't commenced yit to throw hard," replied Poke.

"Wha-at?" yelled Cas. "Are you kidding me? Slam the ball! Break your arm then!"

The rustic whirled a little farther round, unwound himself a little quicker, and swung his arm. Cas made an ineffectual attempt to hit what looked like a white cord stretched between him and the pitcher. The next ball started the same way, but took an upward jump and shot under Cas's chin.

Cas, who had a mortal dread of being hit, fell back from the plate and glared at Poke.

"You've got his alley, Poke!" cried the amiable players. "Keep 'em under his chin!"

Cas retired in disgust as Mac came trotting up from the field, where he had been coaching the high school player.

"What's he got?" asked Mac eagerly.

"What's he got!" yelled nine voices in unison. "Oh! nothing!"

"Step up an' take a turn," said Mac to his new player. "No, don't stand so far back. Here, let me show you. Gimme the bat."

Mac took a position well up to the plate and began illustrating his idea of the act of hitting.

"You see, I get well back on my right foot, ready to step foward with my left. I'll step just before he delivers the ball. I'll keep my bat over my shoulder an' hit a little late, so as to hit to right field. Thet's best for the hit-an'-run game. Now, watch. See. Step an' set; step an' set. The advantage of gettin' set this way is the pitcher can't fool you, can't hit you. You needn't never be afraid of bein' hit after you learn how to get set. No pitcher could hit me."

Then raising his voice, Mac shouted to Poke, "Hey, poke up a couple. Speed 'em over, now!"

Poke evidently recognized the cardinal necessity of making an impression, for he went through more wonderful gyrations than ever. Then he lunged forward with the swing he used in getting the ball away. Nobody saw the ball.

Bumb! A sound not unlike a suddenly struck bass drum electrified the watching players.

Then the ball appeared rolling down from Mac's shrinking person. The little manager seemed to be slowly settling to the ground. He turned an agonized face and uttered a long moan.

"My ribs! my ribs!—he hit me," gasped Mac.

Chase, Poke, and the new man were the only persons who did not roll over and over on the ground.

That incident put an end to the morning "drill."

After dressing, Chase decided to try to find

88

Mittie-Maru. The mascot had not been at the last two games, and this fact made Chase determined to seek out the lad. So he passed down the street where he had often left Mittie and asked questions on the way. Everybody knew the hunchback, but nobody knew where he lived. Chase went on until he passed the line of houses and got into the outskirts of the town, where carpenter shops, oil refineries, and brickyards abounded. Several workmen he questioned said they saw the boy almost every day, and that he kept on down the street toward the open country. Chase had about decided to give up his quest, when he came to the meadows and saw across them the green of a line of willows. This he knew marked a brook or river, along which a stroll would be pleasant.

When he reached the river he saw Mittie-Maru sitting on a log patiently holding a long crooked fishing pole.

"Any luck?" he shouted.

Mittie-Maru turned with a start and, seeing Chase, cried out, "You ole son-of-a-gun! Trailed me, didn't you? What yer doin' out here?"

"I'm looking for you, Mittie."

"What fer?"

Chase leaped down the bank and seated himself on the log beside the boy.

"Well, you haven't been out to the grounds lately. Why?"

"Aw! nuthin'," replied Mittie savagely.

"See here, you can't fool me," said Chase earnestly. "Things aren't right with you, Mittie, and you can't bluff me about it. So I've been hunting you. We're going to be partners, you know."

"Are we?"

Chase then saw Mittie's eyes for the first time, and learned they were bright, soft, and beautiful, giving his face an entirely different look.

"Sure. And that's why I wanted to find you—where you lived—and see if you were sick again."

"It's my back, Chase," replied Mittie reluctantly. "Sometimes it—hurts worse."

"Then it pains you all the time?" asked Chase, voicing a suspicion that had come to him from watching the boy.

"Yes. But it ain't bad today. Sometimes—hol' on! I got a bite. See! It's a whopper—thunder! I missed him!"

Mittie-Maru rebaited his hook and cast it into the stream. "Fishin' fer mine, when I can't git to the ballgrounds! Do you like fishin', Chase?"

"Love it. You must let me come out and fish with you."

"Sure. There's good fishin' fer catfish an' suckers, an' once in a while a bass. I never fished any before I came here, an' I missed a lot. You see, movin' around ain't easy for me. Gee! I can walk, but I mean playin' ball or any games the kids play ain't for me. So I take mine out in fishin'. I've got so I like sittin' in the sun with it all lonely aroun', 'cept the birds an' ripples. I used to be sore— about—about my back an' things, but fishin' has showed me I could be worse off. I can see an' hear as well as anybody. There! I got a bite again!"

Mittie-Maru pulled out a sunfish that wriggled and shone like gold in the sunlight.

"Thet's enough fer today. I ain't no fish-hog. Chase, if I show you where I live you won't squeal? Of course you won't."

Chase assured him he would observe absolute secrecy; and together they mounted the bank and walked upstream. The meadows were bright with early June daisies and buttercups; the dew had not yet dried from the clover; blackbirds alighted in the willows and larks fluttered up from the grass. They came presently to an abandoned brickyard, where piles of broken brick lay scattered around, and two moundlike kilns stood amid the ruins of some frame structures.

"Here we are," said Mittie-Maru, marching up to one of the kilns and throwing open a rudely contrived door. A dark aperture revealed the entrance to this singular abode.

"You don't mean you live in this oven?" ejaculated Chase.

"Sure. An' I've lived in worse places. Come in, an' make yourself at home."

Mittie-Maru crawled into the hole, and Chase followed him. It was roomy inside. Light came in from the chimney hole in the roof, and also on one side where there was a crack in the bricks. The floor was clean and of smooth sand. A pile of straw and some blankets made Mittie-Maru's bed. A fireplace of bricks, a few cooking utensils, and a box cupboard told that he was his own housekeeper.

"This's not bad. How long have you lived in here?"

"Aw, I fooled around town fer a while last summer, spendin' my money fer swell lodgin's, an' then I found this place. Makes a hit with me."

"But when you're sick, Mittie, what do you— how do you manage?"

"Out of sight, an' I ain't no bother to no one."

And that was all Mittie-Maru would vouchsafe concerning himself. They came out after a while and Chase wanted to walk farther up the river. Rolling meadows stretched away to the hills; there was a grove of maples not far off.

"It's so pretty up that way. Can't we go farther on and strike another road into town?"

"Sure. But them meadows an' groves is private property," said Mittie dubiously. "I used to fish up thet way, till I threw Miss Marjory down; then I quit. She lives in one of them grove houses. We ain't likely to meet no one, though, so come on."

They crossed several fields to enter the grove. The river was narrow there and shaded by big trees. Violets peeped out of the grass. A white house gleamed in the distance.

Suddenly they came around a huge spreading tree to a green embankment. A boat rode in the water, one end lightly touching the sand. And in the boat was a girl. Her eyes were closed; her head rested on her arm, which hung over the side. A mass of violets lay in her lap. All about the boat was deep shade, but a gleam of sunshine, filtering through the leaves, turned the girl's hair to gold.

Mittie-Maru uttered a suppressed exclamation and bolted behind some bushes. Chase took a step to follow suit, when the girl opened her eyes and saw him. She gave a little cry, which rooted Chase to the spot.

Then because of the movement of the girl the boat left the sand and drifted into the stream. Whereupon Mittie-Maru returned valiantly to the scene.

"Miss Marjory! Don't be scared. It's all right. We'll get you in. Where's the oars? Chase, you'll hev to wade in. The water ain't deep. Come here, the boat's goin' close to this sandbar."

Chase became animated at Mittie's words and, hurriedly slipping off his shoes and stockings, he jumped to the sand below and waded out. Deeper and deeper the water grew, till he was far over his knees. Still the boat was out of reach. He could tell by feeling with his foot that another step would plunge him over his head, and was about to swim, when Mittie came to the rescue.

He threw a long pole down to Chase.

"There! let her grab that, an' pull her in."

Chase extended the pole, and as the girl caught it he saw her eyes. They were dark blue and smiled into his.

"Careful!" shouted the pilot above. "Don't pull so hard, Chase, this ain't no tug-o'-war. There! All right!"

When Chase moored the boat Miss Marjory gathered up the violets and lightly stepped ashore. Then an obvious constraint affected the three. She murmured a low "Thank you," and stood, picking the flowers; Chase bent over his shoes and stockings with a very flushed face, and Mittie-Maru labored with sudden and painful emotions.

"Miss Marjory, it 'peared like we pushed the boat out, me an' Chase, but thet ain't so. We was walkin' this way—he wanted to go in the grove—an' all at onct we spied you, an' I ducked behind the bushes."

"Why? Are you afraid of me, Mittie-Maru?" she asked.

"Yes—no—it ain't thet, Miss Marjory. Well, no use lyin'. I've been keepin' out of your way fer a long time now, 'cause I know you'd have me in Sunday school."

"Now you will come back, won't you?"

"I s'pose so," he said with resignation, then looked at Chase. "Miss Marjory, this's my friend Chase, Findlay's new shortstop."

"I met the—new shortstop last week," was the demure reply.

"Miss Marjory, you didn't sell Chase none of them gold bricks at the church sociable?"

"No, Mittie, but I sold him five plates of ice cream," she answered with a merry laugh. "Your friend has forgotten me."

Mittie-Maru regarded Chase with a fine contempt. Chase was tongue-tied. Somewhere he had indeed seen those deep blue eyes; they were like the memory of a dream.

"Miss—Miss—" stammered Chase.

"Miss Dean, Marjory Dean."

"I met—so many girls—I didn't really have time—to get to know—anybody well—"

Mittie-Maru watched them with bright, sharp eyes, and laughed when Chase broke into embarrassed speech again.

"—finest time I ever had. I told Mittie about it, how they sold me a lot of old maid's things. I sent some of them to my mother. And I asked Mittie if he could use a pincushion or two. I've been hunting Mittie all morning. Found him fishing down here. He's got the cutest little den in a kiln at the old brickyard below. He lives there. It's the coziest place—"

Mittie had administered to Chase a series of violent kicks, the last of which had brought him to his senses.

"Chase, you peached on me. You give me away, an' you said you wouldn't!"

"Oh! Mittie, I'm sorry—I didn't think," cried Chase in contrition.

"Is it true?" asked Marjory with grave eyes.

"Sure. An' I don't mind yer knowin'. Really I don't, if you'll promise not to tell a soul."

"I promise. Will you let me come to see you?"

"I'd be tickled to death. You an' Chase come to call on me. I'll ketch you a mess of fish. Won't thet be fine?"

Marjory's long lashes fell. The sound of a bell came ringing through the grove.

"That's for me. I must be going. Good-bye."

Chase and Mittie watched the slight blue-clad figure flit along the path, in and out among the trees, to disappear in the green.

"An' I promised to go to Sunday school again," muttered Mittie-Maru.

NINE

ON THE ROAD

AT six o'clock on the twelfth of June the Findlay baseball club, fifteen strong, was assembled at the railroad station to begin a two weeks' trip on the road. Having taken three games from Columbus, and being now but a few points behind that team, they were an exceedingly lively company of young men. They were so exuberant with joy that they made life a burden for everybody, particularly for Mac. The little manager had trouble enough at home, but it was on the road that he got his gray hairs.

"Sure, Cas, you ain't after takin' thet dog again?" asked Mac.

Castorious had a vicious-looking beast, all head and jaws, under his arm.

"Dog!" roared Cas, insulted. "This's a blooded bull-terrier pup. 'Course I'm going to take him. We can't win the pennant without Algy."

"Algy? Is thet his name?" burst out Mac, who had already exhausted his patience. "That's a fine

97

name for a mongrel brute. He's uglier than a mud fence."

As Mac concluded, a rat ran across the platform. Algy saw it, and with a howl wriggled out of his master's arms and gave chase. The platform was crowded with people, of whom ladies made up the greater part. Algy chased the rat from under the trucks and between the trunks right into the crowd. Instantly a scene of great excitement prevailed. Women screamed and rushed frantically into each others' arms; some fell over their grips; several climbed upon trunks; all of them evinced a terror that must have had its origin in the movements of the escaping rat, not the pursuing pup. And the course of both animals could be marked by a zigzag line of violent commotion in the crowd. Presently a woman shrieked and seemed to sit down upon a moving object only to slip to the floor. Algy appeared then with the rat between his jaws.

"It was a cinch he'd get it," yelled Cas. He gathered up the pup and hid him under his coat.

"Line up! Line up!" shouted Mac as the train whistled.

The players stepped into a compact, wedge-shaped formation; and when the train stopped in the station they moved in orderly mass through the jostling mob. Ballplayers value a rest to tired legs too much to risk standing up, and even in the most crowded stations always board the train first.

"Through to the Pullman!" yelled Mac.

Chase was in the seventh heaven of delight. He had long been looking forward to what the players called "on the road," and the luxurious Pullman suited his dreams of travel. He and Winters took a seat opposite a very stout old lady who gazed somewhat sourly at them. Havil and Thatcher were on the other side of the aisle; Cas had a seat in the forward end; Mac was behind; and the others were scattered about. There were some half dozen passengers besides, notable among whom was a very tall, thin, bald-headed man sitting in front of Havil.

Chase knew his fellow players too well by this time to expect them to settle down calmly. "On the road" was luxury for ballplayers. Fast trains, the best hotels, all expenses paid—these for a winning baseball team were things to appreciate. Chase settled back in the soft-cushioned seat to watch, to see, to enjoy every move and word of his companions.

"Where will we sleep?" he asked Winters.

"Never on a sleeper?"

Chase smiled and shook his head.

Then Enoch began to elaborate on the beds that were let down from the ceiling of the car, and how difficult they were to get into and out of, especially the latter in case of fire, which broke out very frequently on Pullmans.

"An' if anybody yells 'Fire!' you skedaddle to the fire escape," concluded Enoch.

"Fire escape? On a train? Where is it?" queried Chase, wonderingly.

"Don't you know where the fire escape is?" asked Enoch in innocent surprise. His round owl eyes regarded Chase in a most kindly light. "Well, you ask the porter. He'll take an' show you."

Straightaway Chase forgot it in the interest of other things. The train was now in smooth, rapid motion; the fields and groves and farms flashed by. He saw the conductor enter the car and stand by Cas. Cas looked up and then went on calmly reading his paper.

"Tickets," said the conductor sharply.

Cas paid not the slightest attention to him.

"Tickets," repeated the conductor, getting red in the face. He tapped Cas not lightly on the shoulder.

"Wha-at?" demanded Cas.

"Your ticket! I don't wish to be kept waiting. Produce your ticket."

"I don't need a ticket to ride on this bum road."

The conductor looked apoplectic. He reached up to grasp the bell-cord.

"Your ticket, or I'll stop the train and put you off."

"Put me off! I'd like to have a tintype of your whole crew trying to put me off this train."

Mac came into the car, and divining how matters stood, hurried forward to produce his party ticket. The conductor, still in high dudgeon, passed on down the aisle.

"Good evenin', Mr. Conductor, this's fine weather for travelin'," said Enoch, in his soft voice. The conductor glanced keenly at him, but evidently disarmed by the placid round face and kind round eyes, replied in gracious affirmation.

Enoch whispered in Chase's ear, "Wait till the crew finds Cas's bulldog! Don't miss thet!"

Some thirty miles out of Findlay the train stopped at a junction. A number of farmers were lounging around the small station. Enoch raised the window and called one of them.

"Hey! What's the name of this place?" he asked of the one who approached, an angular, stolid rustic in overalls and top boots.

"Brookville, mister," was the civil reply.

"Brookville! Wal, I swan! You don't say! Fellow named Perkins live here?"

"Yep. Hiram Perkins."

"Hiram—Hiram Perkins, my ole friend." Enoch's round face beamed with an expression of benign gratitude, as if he would, were it possible, reward the fellow for his information. "Tell Hiram his ole friend Si Hayrick was passin' through an' sends regards. Wal, how's things? Ploughin' all done? You don't say! An' corn all planted? Do tell! An' the ham-trees growin' all right?"

"Whet?" questioned the farmer, plainly mystified, leaning forward.

"How's yer ham-trees?"

"Never heerd of sich."

"Wal, doggone me! Why, over in Indianer our ham-trees is sproutin' powerful. An' how about bee's knees? Got any bee's knees this spring?"

The rustic stretched his long neck. Then as the train started off Enoch put his head out of the window and called, "Rubberneck! Rubberneck!"

The stout lady in the opposite seat plainly sniffed her disgust at these proceedings on the part of a grown man. His innocent round stare in no wise deceived her. She gave him one withering glance, adjusted her eyeglass, and went on reading. Several times following that, she raised a hand to her face, as if to brush off a fly. But there was no fly. She became restless, laid aside her magazine, and rang for the porter.

"Porter, close the window above. Cinders are flying in on me."

"Window's closed, ma'am," returned the porter.

"Something is most annoying. I am being stung in the face by something sharp," she declared testily.

"Beggin' your pardon, ma'am, you been mistaken. There's no flies or muskeeters in my car."

"Don't I know when I'm stung?"

The porter, tired and crushed, wearily went his way. The stout lady fumed and fussed, and fanned herself with a magazine.

Chase knew what was going on and was at great pains to contain himself. Enoch's solemn owl face was blank, and Havil, who was shooting shot and causing the lady's distress, bent a pale, ministerial countenance over his paper. Chase watched him closely, saw him raise his head at intervals when he turned a leaf of his paper, but could see no movement of his lips. He became aware, presently, when Havil changed his position, that the attack was now to be directed upon the bald-headed man in the forward seat.

That individual three times caressed the white spot on his head, and then looking in the air all about him, rang for the porter.

"Porter, drive the flies out of the car."

"There ain't no flies, sir."

"Don't talk back to me. I'm from Georgia. We have lots of flies there, and I know it when I feel them!"

"You might be from a hotter place than Georgia, sir, fer all I care," replied the porter, turning at the last like a trodden worm.

"I am annoyed, annoyed. Something has been dropping on my head. Maybe it's water. It comes *dot, dot,* like that."

"I 'spect *you're* dotty, sir!" said the porter, moving off. "An' you sure ain't the only dotty passenger this trip."

The bald-headed man resumed his seat. Unfortunately he was so tall that his head reached above the seat, affording a most alluring target for Havil. Chase, watching closely, saw the muscle along Havil's jaw contract, and then he heard a tiny thump as the shot struck much harder than usual. The gentleman from Georgia jumped up, purple in the face, and trembled so that his newspaper rustled in his hand.

"You hit me with something," he shouted, looking at Thatcher, for the reason, no doubt, that no one could associate Havil's sanctimonious expression with an untoward act.

Thatcher looked up in great astonishment from the book in which he had been deeply interested. The byplay had passed unnoticed so far as he was concerned. Besides, he was ignorant of Havil's genius in the shot-shooting line, and he was a quiet fellow, anyway, but quick in temper.

"No, I didn't," he replied.

The Southerner repeated his accusation.

"No, I didn't, but I will jolt you one," returned Thatcher with some heat.

"Gentlemen, this is unseemly, especially in the presence of ladies," interposed Havil, rising with the dignity of one whose calling he appeared to represent. "Most unseemly! My dear sir, calm yourself. No one is throwing things at you. It is only your imagination. I have heard of such cases, and fortunately my study of medicine enables me to explain. Sometimes on a heated car a person's blood will rise to the brain and, probably because of the motion, beat so as to produce the effect of being lightly struck. This is most often the case in persons whose hirsute decoration is slightly worn off—er, in the middle, you know."

The gentleman from the South sputtered in impotent rage and stamped off toward the smoking car.

"Dinner served in the dining car ahead," called out a white-clad waiter; and this announcement hurried off the passengers, leaving the car to the players, who had dined before boarding the train.

Time lagged then. The porter lit the lights, for it was growing dark; four of the boys went into the smoker to play cards, and the others quieted down. After a while the passengers returned from

105

the diner, and with them the porter, who began making up the berths. Chase watched him with interest.

"Let's turn in," said Enoch. "It's a long ride and we'll be tired enough. Some of us must double up, an' I'm glad we're skinny."

Enoch boosted Chase into the upper berth and swung himself up.

"Take off your outer clothes," said Enoch, "an' be comfortable."

Chase found it very snug up there, and he lay back listening to the smooth rush of the train as it sped on into the night. And before long he fell asleep. When he awakened the car was dark, though a faint gray light came through the window above him. He heard somebody walking softly down the aisle and wondered who it could be. The steps stopped. Chase heard a sound at his feet, and rose to see an arm withdrawn between the curtains. He promptly punched Enoch in the side. Enoch groaned and rolled over.

"Some of the boys stealing our shoes," whispered Chase.

"It's the porter wantin' 'em to shine," said Enoch sleepily. Then he raised his head and listened. "Yep, it's the porter. I'm glad you woke me. Now, listen an' you'll hear somethin' funny. Cas always smuggles his bull-pup into the car, an' hides him from the porter, an' then puts him to sleep at the foot of the berth. Thet porter will be after Cas's shoes pretty soon."

At intervals of every few moments the porter's soft footsteps could be plainly heard. He was making toward the upper end of the car.

"It's comin' to him," whispered Enoch tensely.

A loud, savage, gurgling growl burst out in the stillness, and then yells of terror. A terrific uproar followed. Bumpings and bangings of a heavy body in the aisle; sharp whacks and blows; steady, persistent growling; screams of fright from the awakened women; wild peals of delight from the ballplayers; above all, the yelling of the porter—these sounds united to make a din that would have put a good-sized menagerie to the blush.

It ended with the unlucky porter making his escape, and Cas coaxing his determined protector back into the berth. By and by silence once more reigned in the Pullman.

Chase, having had his sleep, lay there as long as he could, and seeing it was broad daylight, decided he would crawl over Enoch and get out of the berth. By dint of some extraordinary exertions he got into his clothes and shoes. Climbing over Enoch was no difficult matter, though he did not accomplish it without awakening him. Then Chase parted the curtains, put his feet out, turned and grasped the curtain pole, and balanced himself momentarily, preparatory to leaping down. The position was awkward for him, and as he loosened his kneehold he slipped and fell. One of his feet went down hard into a very large, soft substance that suddenly heaved like a swelling wave. As Chase rolled into the aisle screams rent the air.

"Help! Help! Thieves! Murder! Murder! Murder!"

He had fallen on the fat woman in the lower berth.

Chase saw a string of heads bobbing out of the curtains above and below, and he heard a mighty clamor that made the former one shrink by comparison.

The conductor, brakeman, and porter rushed in. Chase tried to explain, but what with the wails of the outraged lady and the howls of the players it was impossible to make himself heard. He went away and hid in the smoking car till the train stopped near Steubenville, where they were to change for Wheeling.

When the Findlay team had all stepped off the Pullman, leaving the porter enriched and smiling his surprise, it was plain to Chase that he had risen in the regard of his fellow players.

"Say, Chase, you're coming on!"

"You'll do, old man!"

"It was the best ever!"

"The fire escape, my lad, is not in a lady's berth!"

"Go wan! What you giving us? You kicked her in the stomach jest by accident? Go wan!"

Chase found it impossible to make the boys believe that he had fallen from the upper berth and had stepped on the poor lady unintentionally.

The run along the Ohio to Wheeling was a beautiful one, which Chase thoroughly enjoyed. It was his first sight of a majestic river. During the ride Mac sat beside him and descanted on baseball in general and baserunning in particular.

"Chase, a lad as fast as you ought to make all these catchers crawl under the bench. Now, listen to me. To get away quick is the secret. It's all in the start. Of course, depend some on coachin', but use your head. Don't take too big a lead off the base. Fool the pitcher an' catcher. Make 'em think you ain't goin' down. Watch the pitcher an' learn his motion. Then get your start jest as he begins to move. Before he moves is the time, but it takes practice. Run like a deer, watch the baseman, an' hit the dirt feet first an' twist out of his way. But pick out the right time. Of course when you get the hit-an'-run sign you've got to go. Don't take chances in a close game. I say, don't as a rule. Sometimes a darin' steal wins a game. But there's times to take chances an' times not to. Got thet?"

"Mac, where's the bat sack?" asked one of the players, when they arrived at Wheeling.

"Sure, I forgot it," said Mac blankly. "I'll have to buy some bats."

"You ought to be in a bush league," said one.

"How do you expect us to hit without our bats?" asked another.

"Did you forget my sticks?" cried Thatcher, champion hitter, utterly lost without his favorite bats.

Player after player loomed up over the little manager and threatened him in a way that would have convinced outsiders he had actually stolen the bats. Mac threw up his hands, and in wordless disgust climbed into the waiting bus.

To Chase, riding to the hotel, having dinner, dressing for the game, and then a long bus ride out to the island grounds were details of further enjoyment. Findlay was a great drawing card and the stands were crowded. Chase was surprised to hear players spoken of familiarly, as if they were members of the hometeam. "That's Castorious, the great pitcher." "There's old man Hicks, but say! he can catch some." "See, that's good old Enoch, the coacher." "Where's the new short-stop? The papers say he's a wonder." Chase moved out of hearing then and began picking over

110

the new bats Mac had bought. Enoch came up and looked them over, too.

"Bum lot of sticks," he commented. "Say, Chase, Wheeling is a swell town to play in. The fans here like a good game an' don't care who wins. The kids are bad, though. Look out for them. This's a good ground to hit on. You ought to lambaste a couple today. If Finnegan pitches, you wait for his slowball and hit it over the fence."

Findlay won the game 6 to 1. Castorious was invincible. Dude Thatcher hit one over the right field fence, and Chase hit one over the left field fence. The crowd cheered lustily after each of these long drives.

When the players piled into the bus to ride back to the hotel Chase saw them bundling up their heads in sweaters, and soon divined the cause. His enlightenment came in the shape of a swiftly flying pebble that struck his head and made him see stars. As the bus rolled out of the grounds Chase saw a long lane lined with small boys.

"Whip up your horses, you yahoo!" yelled Cas.

"We're off!" shouted another.

"Duck yer heads! Low bridge! Down with yer noggins!"

Then a shower of stones, mud, apples, and tin cans flew from all sides at the bus. The players fell on the floor and piled upon one another, in every way trying to hide their faces. Chase fell with them and squeezed down as well as he could to avoid the missiles. It was a veritable running of the gauntlet and lasted till the plunging bus had passed the lines and outdistanced the pursuers. Then came the strenuous efforts imperative to untangle a dozen or more youths of supple bodies. Only the fortunate players who had been quick enough to throw themselves to the floor first, had escaped bruises or splotched uniforms, and they were hardly better off because of the smashing they had received.

"Gee! I got a lump on my head, all right," said Chase.

"Thet was sweet as ridin' to slow music. Wait, wait till we strike Kenton."

That evening after supper, while Chase was sitting in front of the hotel, Cas whispered to him to look out for tricks. He spent the evening in and around the lobby and kept his eyes open. Nothing happened, and at ten o'clock he went upstairs to find his room. He unlocked the door and opened it, to be deluged by a flood of water from overhead. Next a bucket fell on him and almost knocked him down. Shivering and thoroughly drenched, he fumbled on the bureau, finally found matches, and struck a light. A bucket, two sticks, and a string lay on the floor in a great pool of water.

"One of the t-tricks," muttered Chase with chattering teeth.

He locked his door, closed and fastened his transom, plugged the keyhole, and then felt reasonably safe. For a long time there were mysterious goings-on in that part of the hotel. Soft steps and subdued voices, snickerings, with occasionally a loud, angry noise, attested to the activity of those who were playing the tricks. Chase finally got to sleep and had a good night's rest. In the morning as he came out from breakfast he found most of his team assembled as usual in the lobby.

"Hev a good night, Chase?" asked several.

"Fine. Little wet, though, early in the evening," replied Chase, joining in the general laugh.

"Watch for Brill. Don't miss it," said somebody.

Brill was one of the pitchers, a good player, quiet in his demeanor, and rather an unknown quantity. He was a slow, easygoing Virginian. Presently he appeared on the stairs, came down, and with pale face and deliberate steps he approached the players.

"Mawnin', boys," he said, in his Southern drawl. "I shore hev somethin' to say to yo' all. I don't mind about the ice water, an' I don't mind about the piller somebody hit me with, but I tell yo' all right hyar, the fellar—who—put—thet—there—leapfrog—in—mah—bed—is—goin'—to—git—licked!"

But Brill never found out who put the leapfrog in his bed. Wild horses could not have dragged the secret from his comrades.

That evening, when the players were sitting in front of the hotel with their chairs tipped back, a slight, shabbily dressed woman with a dark shawl over her head approached and timidly asked for Mr. Castorious.

"Here I am, ma'am. What can I do for you?" replied the pitcher, rising.

"My husband sent me, sir. Jim Ayers he is, sir, an' used to work in Findlay, where he knew you," she said in a low voice. "He wants to know if you'll help him—lend him a little money. We're bad in need, sir—an' I've a baby. Jim, he's been out of work an' only got a job last week, an' the second day he was run over by a team—"

"I read it in the paper," interrupted Cas. "Yes, I remember Jim."

"He said you'd remember him," she went on eagerly. "Jim, he had friends in Ohio. He oughtn't never to have left there. He hasn't done well here—but Jim's the best fellow—he's been good to me—an' never drinks except when he's down on his luck."

Cas gently turned her toward the light. She was only a girl, worn, sad.

"Sure, I remember Jim," said Cas hurriedly. "Fine fellow, Jim was, when he left off drinking.

I'll lend Jim some money, Mrs. Ayers, if you'll promise to spend it on yourself and baby."

The young woman hesitated, then with a wan, grateful smile murmured, "Thank you, sir, I will."

"Now, you just go around the corner and wait." Castorious led her a few steps toward the corner.

When she had gotten out of sight he took a roll of bills from his pocket and, detaching one, put it in his hat.

"Dig up," he said, thrusting the hat under Mac's snub nose.

"Cas, you're easy. You remember Ayers, don't you?" replied Mac.

"I do. He was strictly no good, a booze-fighter, an all-around scamp. I wouldn't give him the price of a drink. But that girl, his wife—did you see her face?"

"I did," growled Mac, with his hand moving slowly toward his pocket.

"Dig up, then."

Mac dug, and generously.

The tall pitcher loomed over Thatcher.

"Can you spare the price of a few neckties to aid a poor woman?" he asked sarcastically.

"I can," instantly replied the Dude, throwing a bill into Cas's hat.

Ballplayers fight out rivalries even in their charities. Cas glanced grandly down on the Dude and then passed to Havil.

115

"The pot's opened for five," he said to Havil. Next to shooting shot, Havil liked best a game of poker. In a flash he had contributed to the growing fund.

"I'm in, and it costs two more to play," he replied.

"Hicks, come on."

"Cas, I'm broke, an' Mac won't give me a cent till Saturday night," answered Hicks.

"Borrow, then," rejoined Cas curtly. He threw his roll of bills into the catcher's lap.

Chase and several of the other players were ready for Cas, and so escaped calumny. Enoch mildly expostulated.

"I'm gettin' tired of bein' buncoed this way," he remarked.

"Produce. Ain't you the captain? Don't you draw the biggest salary? Produce," went on the inexorable Cas.

"But, Cas, you're always helpin' some beggar or other."

"Wha-at!" demanded Cas hotly. "It was only last week you touched the team for a scraggly hobo. Produce!"

Enoch meekly produced.

"Wha's the matter?" inquired Benny, lounging out of the hotel door. As usual he was under the influence of drink.

"Hol' on, Cas—gee! Wha's all the dough for? Lemme in."

"Never mind, Benny," replied Cas. "Just raising a little collection for Jim Ayers' wife. Remember Jim?"

"Got drunk with Jim many a time—hol' on there. Wha's the matter? Is my money counterfeit?"

Benny was the most improvident of fellows. He seldom had any money. And his bad habit excluded him from many of the plans and pleasures of his comrades.

"Say, Benny, this isn't a matter of the price of a beer," replied Cas, moving toward the corner.

Benny straightened up.

"You're only kiddin' me—if I thought you meant that for an insult—say! I'm just as much a sport an' gennelman as you, any day."

Thereupon Benny soberly thrust his hand into his pocket, pulled out a bill and some silver, soberly turned the pocket inside out to get the small change, and with great dignity dropped all the money into Cas's hat.

MARJORY AND POND LILIES

IT was July second, and Chase was happy. Many things had occurred to make him so; summed up, they made a great beautiful whole. The team had won fourteen straight victories before dropping a game to Columbus and had come home in first place. He had kept up his good work, especially at the bat. Friends he had made everywhere. What a rousing welcome Findlay had given its team on homecoming! On the first of the month he had drawn one hundred dollars and had sent it home to his mother. While in Columbus Mac had taken him to see a surgeon, a wonderful specialist, who had injected something into the corner of his crooked eye, had cut a muscle or ligament, and then bound a little black cap over the eye, cautioning him to wear it till a certain time. Chase had managed to play with only one eye, but now the time was up. That morning he had temporarily slipped off the black cap to find he did not recognize the straight-glanced, clear-eyed person in the mirror.

Then there was another thing, which, though he would hardly admit it to his own consciousness, had more than all else added a brightness to his day. An exceptionally large and enthusiastic audience had attended yesterday's game, and in the grandstand, sitting among a merry crowd of young people, he had seen golden hair and blue eyes that he knew. He looked again to make sure. It was Marjory. And the whole grandstand seemed to grow gayer and brighter, the shrill cries of excited rooters had a joyous ring, the very sky and field took on a warmer color. The wonder of wonders was that at a critical stage of the game, when by fast sprinting he scored a run and was passing by the stand, he looked up to catch wonderfully, in all that sea of faces and waving hats, a smile meant for him.

Even the abuse of his fellow players, renewed doubly since the homecoming, had no power to affect him after that smile. And a significant remark of Mittie-Maru's had further enhanced the spell.

"I've fixed it fer you, all right, all right. You mosey out along the river. See!"

Chase had turned hot and cold at Mittie's speech, had lamely questioned him further, but nothing more, except elaborate winks, could be elicited from the mascot.

And all this was why Chase was happy and

119

roaming wild in the meadows. It was a soft, warm summer morning. The larks were turning their black-spotted yellow breasts to the sun and singing their sweet songs. Chase tramped and tramped, and ever resolutely tried to turn away from the maple grove along the river. But every circle led that way, and he found himself at last in the shade of the trees. Through the bushes he caught a glance of the cool river, and then he saw a boat and a glimpse of blue and a gleam of gold. He tried to run away, but could not. His steps led him down the sandy path to the huge old maple.

"Good morning, Mr. Chase. Why, aren't you lost?" Marjory's blue eyes regarded him in laughing surprise.

Chase had a vague thought that somehow he was lost, but all he could think of to say was that the weather was fine for the time of year.

"It is—lovely," she said.

Then he had a brilliant thought, and he wondered why it had not come sooner.

"Were—you going to—row?"

"Oh, yes. I always row every morning."

"Might I—would you—I—I like to row."

"You do? How nice! Then you must row me up to the meadow pond where the lilies grow."

Chase awkwardly got into the boat. Whatever was wrong with his hands and feet? When he had seated himself and straightened the oars he began to row. She was very close to him. He had not looked up, but he saw her little feet and the blue hem of her gown.

"You're rowing into the bank," she said.

"Why—so I am." Hastily he turned out and then was careful to row straight. The boat glided smoothly and silently. The little river meandered between high green banks. Tall trees cast shadows on the water. Here were dark patches of shade, there golden spaces of sunshine. Birds were flitting and singing.

"Have you seen Mittie-Maru?" asked Chase.

"Yes, indeed. Lots of times. I've seen his den and fished with him and we've rowed after pond lilies and had fine times together."

What was there in her simple, kind words to make him feel so strangely toward Mittie? Of course he was glad she had been with Mittie, but somehow the gladness was an entirely new thing. All at once he discovered he was sorry that the Findlay team had to play games on the road. If it had not been for that he could have helped her give Mittie a good time.

"Here's the pond," said Marjory. "It's very shallow, so you must be careful or we'll stick in the mud."

Chase saw that the river widened out into a large basin. There were islands, and bogs, and piles of driftwood. The green and gold and white of pond lilies sparkled on all sides. The place was alive with birds and water denizens. Kingfishers resented the invasion; water-wagtails skimmed the surface and screamed plaintive cries. Turtles splashed off stumps and frogs plunked under the lily pads. Snakes sunned themselves in bright places. And a great gray crane stood solemnly on one leg and watched.

"I want a pink one," said Marjory, after Chase had gathered a mass of dripping lilies. He rowed around the pond, and at last located a lily of the desired color, but could not reach it from the boat. He stepped out upon a log and stretched as far as he could reach.

"Oh! You'll fall in!" cried Marjory in sweet solicitude.

Chase slipped off the log and went in with a great splash. The water came up to his waist. He managed by grasping a branch to avert a worse disaster, and securing the coveted pink lily, climbed back upon the log and so got into the boat.

"You shouldn't have done that," she said.

"It's nothing. I'll dry in a little while."

Then they both laughed. Chase rowed back to the bank and placed the boat so that Marjory was in the shade of an overhanging grapevine, and he sat out in the sun. Somehow her merry laughter had given him courage, so he raised his glance to look at her. She had been only pretty before. Now! But the blue of her eyes meeting his drove away his thoughts.

"When will you be able to—to take off that eye shield?" she asked.

"Why—how did you know?" he asked breathlessly.

"I heard, and I read the baseball news every day."

"You do?" exclaimed Chase. Then he took off the shield and threw it away.

"Oh! I'm glad. But—but are you sure it's time?"

"Yes. I only waited because—well, that is—I—I wanted you to see me first."

This appeared to be an unfortunate remark, for Marjory colored a soft rose under her white cheeks, and began diligently to sort the lilies.

"Mittie-Maru will be glad," said Chase.

"If only he could be cured, too!" she replied. "Do you know he suffers all the time, and sometimes dreadfully, yet he never says a word?"

"Yes, I know. Poor Mittie!" Chase found it much easier to talk, now that she avoided looking at him. "You were at the game yesterday. Do you like baseball?"

"Oh, yes, indeed. I like the running, and I love to see the ball flying, but I don't understand much of the game."

"Won't you let me teach you?"

"Thank you, that would be nice, but I'm so stupid."

"Stupid! You?" Chase laughed at the hint of such an impossibility. A blue flitting gleam flashed upon him from under the long lashes.

"Oh, I am. Now what is a bingo?"

"A bingo? Why, that's baseball talk for a safe hit, a ball knocked safely out of the reach of a fielder."

"What does Captain Winters mean when he hops around the base and yells: 'Mugg's Landing! Irish stew! Ras-pa-tas'?"

"He's coaching then, saying any old thing to try to rattle the pitcher."

"Oh, is that it? What do you do with a base after you steal it?"

"Stealing a base means to run from first to second, or from second to third, without being put out. It really means stealing the distance, not the base."

"What's a foul?"

"A ball hit any way back of the white lines running from homeplate to first and third base."

"What's a knocker? A fellow who gives the ball a knock?"

"That's more baseball talk. A fellow who speaks ill of another is a knocker."

"Oh, but doesn't he play the game too? I heard

Mr. Winters say he was captain and first knocker. I'm surprised about him. He has such a nice face."

"Captain Winters meant he was the first batter."

"Then why did he say he was first knocker? Oh!—you see I'm stupid. I knew you'd seen it."

"I haven't seen it."

"You have. You as much as said so. I won't go to any more games."

The flash of reproachful fire and the glimpse of a petulant face that accompanied the words caused a sinking of Chase's heart. What in the world had he said?

"Marjory—" he cried. Then at the sound of his voice, at his boldness in so addressing her, he halted and began to fumble over his wet shoes and squeeze the water out of his coat. There was a long silence. He dared not look up. How quiet she was! How angry she must be!

"We had better row home," she said at last.

He squared his shoulders and pulled hard on the oars. The little red boat flew over the placid water, leaving a troubled wake. Fast as he rowed he thought it a long way to the maple landing. All the way he never looked up or spoke. He could not think very connectedly; he only knew a terrible calamity had befallen him. He moored the boat and turned to help her out.

Marjory glanced at him over a great load of

pond lilies which she held with both arms. At the very top of the load, just under her lips, lay the pink lily.

"Take it," she said.

"Wh-what?" stammered Chase.

"The pink one."

"Then—it's all right," cried Chase, taking the lily. "We're—you're not angry?"

"Because you said I was stupid? Oh, no."

"I didn't say so. But I meant—about the—"

"You're the stupid one." She tripped up the bank and turned again with her blue gaze shining above the lilies. "I'm having a little party tomorrow night. Will you come?"

"Yes, yes, I'll come—thank you."

"Good-bye."

Then the blue eyes and blue dress were gone. Chase had nothing to prove that they had been there except the pink lily, which he clasped close to make sure of its reality. She had told him to take it, and she meant it to be his. Keep it? Forever! He tramped the meadows like one possessed. The sunlight dazzled him; the river shone like silver; the meadows gleamed white and gold. A glamour lay upon the world. The winds blew sweet in his face. The blue sky came down to meet the horizon like a deep azure curtain. Overhead, all around, sounded a low, soft, steady hum. To him it was music. He ran through the clover field and burst upon Mittie-Maru at his dinner task.

"Mittie, I never was so glad to see you. I've been on the river—been boating—pond lilies. See, this pink one. Isn't it lovely? I fell in trying to reach it. She gave it to me—isn't that great? And we had a quarrel—I called her Marjory, or stupid, or something—we didn't speak for an age—I was sick. Then she gave me this, bless her! And Mittie, she's asked me to her party— it's tomorrow night—she really asked me. Oh!—"

"Say!" yelled Mittie, with all his might. "Cut it out, will you? Hev I been pluggin' yer game with her fer two weeks jest to be mushed over like this? I knew you had it bad, but I'll be dinged if I thought you'd go dotty. You're up in the air. Steady up! Steady up, old man! If you get rattled this way in the first inning, what'll you do when they tie the score along about the fifth? Miss Marjory's got a raft of fellers, as ain't no wonder. An' thet preacher guy I don't like is settin' the pace. Come down out of the air, Chase, me Romeo. Keep cool, play hard, an' along about the eighth, hit one over the fence an' put the game on ice. Now, hev some dinner with yer Uncle Dudley."

ELEVEN

INSIDE BALL

FINDLAY lost the second game to Toledo, and according to Mac, largely through the weird playing by Chase. The *Chronicle* gave the excuse that Chase had not had time to accustom himself to the new arrangement of his eyesight, hence his errors. Mac, however, was not disposed to be generous, and after the game, told Chase he might expect a "call" when there was time to give it. And the players had heaped such terms of reproach upon Chase that he was well nigh distracted. He felt the cardinal necessity of acting on Castorious's advice, yet was loath to bring matters to such an issue.

On the day following, when he presented himself at the grounds, he met Mittie-Maru at the dressing room entrance. It was evident that Mittie wanted to speak to him, but had only time for a warning glance before the explosion came from the players.

Chase walked to his locker through a storm of abuse, and somehow he sensed this was the climax. He turned his back, hurriedly got out his suit, and began to dress. If it must come to a fight he preferred to fight in his uniform. He listened to the storm, and for moments could scarcely distinguish any particular player's voice or epithet. Then suddenly he heard mention of a boat and a girl in such manner that his blood leaped through him like a flame.

The moment had come. He was on his feet trembling.

"Hold on!" he yelled. "I know you're after me. But come now, one at a time—unless you're cowards!"

A blank silence followed his words. Castorious slowly separated himself from the others. Enoch glanced keenly at Chase and said,

"I'm called, sonny. I was only kiddin'."

Chase eyed the next player, who happened to be Havil.

"Me, too," he said.

"I only said you're a swelled-up mutt," put in Thatcher with a disarming smile.

"Aw, you're gittin' too exclusive since thet hoodoo lamp was fixed; too handsome, by far," said Ziegler.

"Go wan, Molly!"

"You make me sick!"

"Willie-off-the-yacht!"

Meade was the next player upon whom Chase

fixed his flashing eyes. The first baseman evidently enjoyed the situation for he sneered and took a couple of steps in Chase's direction. He looked mean.

"Throwin' a bluff, eh? Well, you can't bluff me. You're a pie-faced towhead, that's what you are. Been shuttin' your eyes an' gettin' a few lucky hits—then swell up. See! Mama's little baby boy! Too nice to smoke a cigar or take a drink, eh? But you play around with the girls, you good-for-nothing! Boat ridin', eh? I know the girl, all right. She's one of your dyin'-duck-in-a-thunderstorm kind. She's—"

Chase struck out with all his strength. Meade crashed down into a corner, rolled over, twisted his body, but could not rise. Chase stood over him a moment, then turned round to encounter Benny. As usual, the second baseman was partially drunk, and being a friend of Meade's, he leered threateningly at Chase and raised his arm. Chase promptly slapped him. Benny staggered, lost his balance, and tumbled over a chair. Then he set up a howl. Cas ran to him and helped him to his feet and held on to him.

"Cas, lemme—go. I been hit," howled Benny.

"No, you haven't. But you will git hit in a minute if you don't look out," said Cas.

At that moment Mac came into the dressing

room. Some of the boys were helping Meade to rise, and once up he presented a sorry spectacle. His lip was puffed out and bloody. Benny was now in tears, and crying he had no "frens."

"What's all this—a scrap?" questioned Mac.

Chase briefly told him the circumstances, and concluded in this manner, "Stood it as long as I could. And I want to say right here—if anybody gets after me again he'll be sorry!"

"Sure, it was about time you broke out," growled Mac. "Meade, you got what was comin' to you, an' from the looks of your mug you got it good. You can take thet uniform off. I'm sorry to turn you down, but business is business. You don't fit in with Findlay. I think you might get on with Wheeling, for they like your work down there. You've overdrawn, but let it go et thet."

"An' say, Meade, take a tip from me," chirped in Mittie-Maru. "You're a crack fielder an' a fair sticker, an' you know the game. But you're a knocker. Get wise! Get wise!"

Meade lost no time in getting out of his suit. To the other players his release was but an incident in baseball experience; they all said a good word to him as he was on his way out, and then straightaway forgot him. Cas was remonstrating with Benny. It appeared Benny could not get over the idea that he must fight Chase.

131

"But, Benny, you'll get all beat up," protested Cas. "Because if you lick Chase, which isn't likely, I'll have to lick you myself."

This put an entirely different light on the subject. Benny began to cry again, and said, "Everybody but me hash frens."

"Cut it out! You're half full, I tell you. Brace up, or Mac will be letting you go, too. I'm your friend. So's Chase. Here, Chase, shake hands with Benny. He thinks you've got it in for him."

Chase readily offered his hand, which Benny grasped and worked as if it were a pump handle. He seemed as anxious to be friends as he had been to fight.

"Benny," said Mac, "you're shaky today. I want you to cut this boozin' out. Mind, I'll let you go if you don't. Now, get a little sleep before the game."

Ford, the local player whom Mac was training, now came in for a talk from the manager.

"Here, Ford, an' you, Chase. It won't hurt you to listen. Ford, most of the balls thrown in any game go to first base, an' you must always be there. Practice gettin' back to the base fast. The farther you can play off the base an' still get back, the better you'll be. Play deep when there's no one on the bases. Let the pitcher cover the base sometimes when you're fieldin' a hard chance, an' snap the ball to him underhand. With a runner on first, keep your eye peeled on the hitter. If he bunts down the first base line, you dig for the ball an' peg it to second, an' then hustle back to your base. A fast man gets in double plays thet way. Think sharp, throw quick! Now, on handlin' low throws, if you practice so you can pick up any kind of a bad throw, you will save many a game, an' you will steady up the other infielders. Nothin' helps a fielder so much as to know he can cut loose an' thet you'll get any kind of a throw. You've got a long reach, so don't leave the base in reachin' for wild throws till you have to. Keep both feet before the base, so as to be able to touch it with either foot. An' reach toward the ball as far as you can. The sooner you catch it, the sooner the runner is out. Got thet?

"Now, Chase, a word with you. Thet was a weird game you put up yestiddy. Mind wasn't on the game. See! You was countin' your money, or somethin' like. Mebbe this talk about your bein' spoony has somethin' in it. Anyway, you brace! Mind, you're the keystone of the diamond. If you fall down—smash! You've got to play second an' third as well as short. You've got to think before the play comes off. You've got to take many balls on the run. The particular thing yestiddy was your failure to catch the signals between Hicks an' Benny. Twice you'd have saved runs if you'd caught the signal. Now, today, when Hicks signals

Benny thet he's goin' to try to catch the runner off second, you back up the play. Got thet?"

Mac then turned to the others of his team. "Say, Indians, I'm goin' to pitch Poke today, an' I want you all to get up an' dust."

"Wha-at?" roared Castorious, with his underlip protruding. "I'm going to work today."

"Sure, Cas, you can't pitch all the games. I want to save you. There's the mornin' game on the Fourth with Kenton. We have to go over to Kenton for thet, an' we want to win it. We come back here for the afternoon game, an' I think Speer's good for it. What's agin tryin' Poke today?"

"He's crazy."

"Don't put the Rube in."

"He's wilder than a Texas steer."

These and sundry other remarks expressed the players' opinion as to Mac's new find.

"Well, he goes in, all right," returned Mac. "An' say, you fellers listen to this. Don't any of you lay down. We want thet pennant. The directors have promised us a banquet, a purse, an' a benefit game if we land the flag. Got thet?"

A chorus of exclamations greeted Mac's news.

"An' say, Beekman has put up an extra hundred for the leadin' hitter. Got thet?"

Another howl from the players answered him.

"An' say, King has put up an extra hundred for the leadin' fielder. Got thet?"

This time there was a louder howl.

"An' say, Guggenheimer and Company have put up an extra hundred for the leadin' pitcher. Got thet?"

Cas began to dance and sing. "Do-diddle-de-dum-dum-do-diddle-de. Oh! I don't know. I guess maybe I haven't that extra hundred in my inside pocket right now."

"An' say, if we land the buntin' this season we'll all have to get new trunks to carry away the suits an' hats an' shoes that's promised. Got thet?"

Cas, Benny, Enoch, and the others formed a ring around Poke and danced in Indian fashion.

"Hey! you rail-splitter, if you lose today we'll kill you!"

"Sonny, get them hayseeds out of your eyes!"

"Listen to this, fellows," yelled Cas, breaking up the ring.

> "Reuben, Reuben, we've been thinking
>   That we'll put the kibosh on you
> If today you don't put 'em over,
>   And cut the plate right in two."

Chase found himself joining lustily in the song. There was a scene of wild excitement, which for no apparent reason centered about poor bewildered Poke. The boys sang and yelled at him and slapped him on the back till they were all out of breath.

"Rube, you're on."

"Git in the game now, you long, lanky, scared-lookin' beanpole!"

On the way out, Chase, dazed at himself, not understanding why he had joined in the unanimous attack on Poke, slipped up to him and whispered, "Don't mind it. We mean well. Keep your nerve and pitch hard."

The bleachers showed a disposition to resent Mac's choice in such an important game, and were not slow in voicing their feelings.

"Mac, where did you get it?"

"Lock the gate! Lock the gate!"

"Get some straw for the calves of its legs!"

"Help! Help! Help! Help!"

"Well! Well! Well!"

Poke undoubtedly showed nervousness when he faced the first Toledo batter, and he was wild. He drove the batter back from the plate and then gave him his base on balls. The bleachers broke out in a roar. But the Findlay players then showed one of the beautiful features of baseball, a thing that makes the game what it is.

Hicks walked toward the pitcher, and handing him the ball said, "Ease up! Ease up! Pitch fer my mitt! Take more time!"

Then from all the players came soft, aggressive encouragement.

"Make 'em hit, sonny," said Enoch. "Remember there's seven men back here playin' with you."

"Don't let any more walk, old man," said Ford.

"There's a stone wall behind you, Pokie, so put 'em over," said Benny.

"Let them hit to me," said Chase.

From the outfield came low calls of similar import.

Poke's heart swelled in his throat, as could be seen by the way he swallowed. He was white and dripping with sweat. His perturbation was so manifest that the Toledo players jeered at him. His situation then was the most important and painful stage in the evolution of a pitcher. Much depended on how he would meet it. He threw the ball toward the next batter, who hit it back at him. Poke made a good stop of the ball, dropped it, recovered it, and then stood helpless. Both runners were safe. The Toledo players yelled; the bleachers roared; Poke's chance shone a little dimmer.

Again the Findlay players voiced their characteristic inspiriting calls. Poke threw off his cap and again faced a batter.

"Stay with 'em till your hair blows out!" called Enoch.

The batter hit the next ball sharply to Chase. He was on it with a leap, picked it up cleanly, touched second base on the run, and whipped it to first, making a double play. The runner on second had of course reached third.

"Two down, old man!"

"Play the hitter!"

"Make him hit!"

Toledo's man drove a long fly in Thatcher's direction. As he ran to get under it, the bleachers yelled, "In the well! In the well!" Past experience had taught them what fate to expect of a flyball hit to the Dude.

For Findlay, Enoch went out on a foul to the catcher; Thatcher had two strikes called, missed the next, and retired in disgust; Chase, now batting third, worked a base on balls. A passed ball sent him to second. Then Havil hit sharply through short.

Chase started for third with all his speed. The play was for him to score. When he reached third he was going like the wind. As he circled around the base, Budd, the Toledo third baseman, stuck out his hip. Chase collided with it, went hurtling through the air, and rolled over and over. He felt a severe pain, and the field whirled around. He could not make a move before Budd got the ball and touched him out.

Mac and Enoch came running, and the former spoke some hot words to Budd.

"Wot you givin' us?" said that individual. "Didn't he run agin me? Go soak your head!"

Enoch was bending over Chase. Mittie ran out with a cup of water, and other players surrounded them.

"I'm not hurt much, I guess," said Chase. "I'm only dizzy. Wait a minute. What did he do to me?"

"Call time," yelled Mac to the umpire. "Chase, I told you to look out for Budd. Thet's his old trick. He gave you the hip. Stuck out his hip an' spilled you all over the field. It's a dirty trick, an' a bad thing for a fast man to run agin. I hope you ain't hurt. Sure, you did tumble—won't forgit thet in a hurry."

"Say, Budd, why don't you ever try that on me?" demanded Cas.

"Bah!" replied Budd and walked toward the bench.

Chase was considerably shaken up and bruised, but able to go on with the game. He did not say another word about it, only he made a mental reservation that he would surprise Mr. Budd the next time he rounded third base.

Some snappy fielding saved Poke again in the second inning, and in the third Toledo made a run on a base on balls, a hit, and a fly to the outfield. Then the long-legged pitcher seemed to settle down and lose his nervousness. Thereafter he mowed the Toledo batters down as if they had been cornstalks on his farm. The harder he worked, the swifter he threw, the steadier he became. He was ungainly, he did not know how to pitch, but what speed he had! The fickle bleachers atoned for their derision, the grandstands showed their delight; and the Findlay players, one and all, kept talking to him, lauding him to the skies, and belittling the hitters who faced him.

"Oh! I don't know! Pretty poor, I guess not!"

"Poke 'em over, Poke!"

"Speed! Oh, no! You can't see 'em!"

"Grand, Rube, grand!"

In the eighth inning, when Findlay came in for their turn at bat, Chase ran into the dressing room and searched for a horseshoe nail that he remembered seeing. He put it in his pocket. There was one man out when he came to the bat, and he determined to get his base. As luck would have it he placed a hot single in right field. As soon as he reached first and stopped he took the horseshoe nail out of his pocket and held it firmly in his left hand, point exposed.

One glance toward the bench gave him the sign. Mac's scorecard was in sight, which meant to run on the first ball pitched. Chase watched the Toledo pitcher with hawklike eyes. He got up on his toes and as the pitcher started to swing, Chase started for second base. He heard the crack of a ball as Havil hit it, and he saw it shoot out over short to bound between the running fielders.

He ran as he had never run before, turned second, raced for third, and gripped his horseshoe nail. Budd was leisurely backing into third base trickily, to get there just at the right instant. Chase sped onward, with his eye on that muscular hip. He saw it suddenly, like a gray flash, protrude in his path, and using all his force he swung upward with the horseshoe nail.

Budd sprang spasmodically into the air.

"*Aa-gh!*" A hoarse yell escaped him.

The crowd in the stands and bleachers did not know what Chase had done, but as he easily scored, while Budd walked Spanish, they divined the triumph of retaliation, and howled with all the might of fair-minded lovers of sport.

But the Findlay players and the Toledo players knew how the little youngster Chase had "got back" at the veteran Budd. It was a play such as every ballplayer reveled in. It embodied the great spirit of the game. And to a man they broke out and pranced over the field in unbridled joy. For a time the game was interrupted.

And the best part of the incident was when, after Findlay had won 7 to 3, Budd went into the Findlay dressing room and said to Chase, "Kid, shake hands. I've been lookin' fer thet fer years."

TWELVE

POPULARITY

SMALL boys ushered in the Fourth of July with a bang. The noise began at daybreak, and at nine o'clock when the ballteam left for Kenton, it was in full blast. A trainload of happy enthusiasts accompanied the team. Small boys without tickets hid under the seats, with determination in their hearts and hearts in their throats. And the conductor, being a boy himself that morning, with a wager on Findlay, saw nothing.

"Five hundred strong we're goin' over," said Mac, rubbing his hands. "Sure we'll draw down a big slice of gate money today."

"Rotten arrangement, this mornin' game at Kenton," growled his players. "Kenton is bad enough on any day. But the Fourth! Oh, Lord! What they'll do to us!"

"We can't win," continued Cas, pessimistically. "We'll be dodgin' giant firecrackers, mark what I say!"

When they bowled into the Kenton grounds and poured out of the bus, an enormous shirt-sleeved crowd roared a welcome that was defiance. Then waiting showers of red firecrackers began to fly, and the scene became a smoke-clouded battlefield. Small guns popped incessantly and artillery worked strenuously. When this explosion subsided and the smoke rolled away, the Findlay team stood covered with little red-and-yellow pieces of paper and sniffing the brimstone in the air.

"Git in an' scrap today, boys," cried Enoch, and for once his voice was not soft.

"There's nothing to it," said Cas, forgetting his prophecy.

"A short, hard practice now," added Mac. "Start the dust! Dig 'em up an' peg 'em! Keep lively an' noisy!"

Kenton was very different from Wheeling, being one of those baseball towns where the patrons of the game could not see a point, or appreciate a play, or applaud a game unless it was won by their own team. This operated to the poor showing of their team, because when opposing teams visited Kenton they were driven to desperation by the criticism and taunts and atmosphere of an unsportsmanlike crowd, and they fought the games to the last ditch.

Mac particularly warned his players not to question a single decision of the umpire. That official, "Silk" O'Connor, reported to be as

smooth as silk, was to be making the calls that
day. Silk was the best umpire in the league. But
he was not especially beloved in Kenton. He had
officiated in too many games lost by one run. And
Silk had an irritating habit of adding a caustic
comment to some of his rulings, a kind of wit that
did not inspire the players to silence. Further,
which seemed unreasonable, he never allowed a
player to talk back to him.

"Look out for Silk today, boys," concluded
Mac. "He's up agin it here, same as we are. Don't
expect no close decisions. Don't even look at him.
Jest drive these Kenton pitchers to the woods.
Make the game one-sided."

"Play ball!" called Silk.

Enoch had scarcely reached the batter's box
when the Kenton pitcher delivered the ball.

"Strike!" called Silk, then in low voice, "Foggy
eye."

Another ball came speeding up.

"Strike two!—up late last night?"

Enoch's round face grew red, and the lump in
his cheek swelled out. He slammed at the next
ball and sent it safely past the third baseman.

Thatcher hurried up and took his position on
the left side of the plate.

"Strike!" called Silk. "Hair brushed fine,
Dude!"

Thatcher bunted the next ball and dashed for

first. The pitcher fielded the ball and overthrew, letting Enoch go to third and Thatcher to second.

"Don't wait!" whispered Mac to Chase. "Bing the first good one!"

Chase did bing one, and that with a vengeance. He had the ability to line the ball. This particular hit seemed to be going straight into the hands of the center fielder, but just before reaching him it sailed up and shot over his head.

"*Oh-h!*" yelled Cas, on the coaching line. "Take your time, Enoch. Slow down, Dude, it's easy. Oh, my! I guess it wasn't a beaut. Come on! Come on! Come on! Slide, Chase, slide. That's the way to hit the ground."

Havil hit a high fly to an outfielder. Chase leaned forward and watched the ball till it landed in the fielder's hands; then he darted for the plate. The fielder threw quickly, making a fine race between ball and runner. But Chase had never yet been thrown out on such a play. He slid over the plate just as the ball sped into the catcher's hands.

The game progressed. Kenton came in for their inning and failed to score. Castorious was in rare form; on a hot day his arm was like India rubber. Findlay added one run in the second and again blanked their opponents. In the third Chase got his second hit, and three hits following his, coupled with a base on balls and two errors, netted three more runs. Again Cas foiled the Kenton

145

batters, and the impatient crowd stamped. In the fifth, two Kenton players hit safely with one out. The crowd began to howl. Hicks snapped the ball to Benny, who tagged the runner trying to get back to second.

"*Out!*" called Silk.

The Kenton players ran in a body for the umpire. The grandstand raged; the bleachers rose as one man.

"He's safe! He's safe!"

"Robber! Robber!"

"Kill him! Kill him!"

Silk ordered the players back to the bench. Cas struck out the next two batters and elicited another storm from the bleachers. Someone threw a huge firecracker at Cas.

"*Boom!*" It exploded like a bursting cannon. Cas shook his fist at the bleachers, and that brought forth a rain of smaller firecrackers.

Enoch went up and had a strike called on him. He looked at Silk, and made a motion with his hand to indicate the ball had passed wide of the plate.

"Strike two!" called Silk imperturbably.

Enoch glared at him.

"Strike three!" called Silk, more imperturbably. "You're out!"

Enoch leaned gracefully on his bat, spat tobacco juice about six yards, and said in his soft voice:

"Do you know a ball when you see it?"

"That costs you five dollars," sang out Silk.

"Make it ten, you mullet!"

"Why, Enoch, how sweet you talk! Ten it is!"

"Make it fifteen, pinhead!"

"Dear me, the older you get the more you gab! Fifteen it is!"

"Make it twenty, you web-footed bat!"

"Twenty it is, and out of the game! The bench for yours!"

Enoch roared something in inarticulate rage.

"Get out of the grounds!" ordered Silk. And he held his watch till Enoch shouldered his bat and left the field. Mac threw up his hands as if he knew the game was all over then.

But even without their captain and third baseman, Findlay kept blanking Kenton. In the eighth Cas went to the bat. A silence ensued that seemed to presage some striking event. It came in the shape of a huge red firecracker that tumbled over and over in the air and, dropping behind Cas, exploded with a terrific report, tearing the seat out of his trousers.

Cas jumped about eight feet and then, transformed into a veritable demon, brandishing his bat and roaring like a mad bull, he made for the bleachers.

If Mac and several policemen had not intercepted him, the scene might have passed from comedy to tragedy. As it was, all Cas could do was to wave his fist at the hooting bleachers and yell, "I can lick the man who threw that!"

"Boo! Boo! Redhead! Redhead!"

"I can lick you all," bawled Cas, foaming at the mouth.

In the prevailing excitement the Findlay supporters naturally and foolishly poured out of the stands upon the field. Silk promptly called the game 9 to 0 in Kenton's favor. Then began one of those familiar scenes common to a baseball crowd on the glorious Fourth. Like water the Kenton spectators spilled themselves into the melee. What with the angry altercations between partisans of the teams, and yells and horn-blowing and shooting of the winners, and pushing, jostling, crowding of both sides, the affair bid well to degenerate into a real fight. But this did not happen. It almost never happens. Great rivalry, great provocation never yet spoiled the fair spirit of the game.

But the Findlay players ran a not-soon-to-be-forgotten gauntlet to the railroad station. Sore were they, particularly Cas, who was not able to sit down on the way home; and threatening were the supporters, but by the time the gong rang for the afternoon game in Findlay, resentment vanished in present enjoyment.

For the attendance was very large, the afternoon perfect, and the game a spirited and thrilling one. Only a single misplay marred the brilliant fielding. Both pitchers kept the hitting down. The final score was 2 to 1 in Findlay's favor. Chase's star rose higher; and if there were any who did not admit his popularity before the game, there were none after. For at the right time, at the one great absorbing climax, at the moment when eyes flashed, hands clenched, and hearts almost stopped beating, he performed the unexpected feat, the one thing absolutely glorious to the hoping, despairing audience—he drove the ball far over the fence.

That hit settled it. Never had there been one like it save Dan Brouthers's great and memorable drive of years gone by. Mac threw up his hands and stared in rapture at his star. The crowd carried Chase off the field.

When a player became the idol of the fans it meant something; but when a player made fans out of staid businessmen, and young society men, and girls in school, and women prominent in town and church affairs, then it meant a great deal. It meant money in the box office; support for the team; willing, eager, working baseball champions.

And such a wave carried the Findlay team to the top of popularity, with Chase on the very crest. He was the recipient of more presents in the way of suits, hats, shoes, canes, umbrellas than he knew what to do with. He received a beautiful gold watch, with his monogram engraved on it. He was asked to luncheon with prominent businessmen; he was invited everywhere. And last, a photographer lured him into his den, there took his picture, and reproducing it on small buttons, sold them by the hundreds. Every youngster and almost every girl in town proudly wore Chase's picture. He was public property.

This latter fact became a source of pain to Chase. One day Mittie-Maru, having met Marjory by the river, had enlarged upon this matter of the picture buttons, with the result that he had interesting news for Chase.

"She wouldn't hev one! Wot do you think of thet? Said you were conceited to allow 'em sold. Somehow she blamed you fer it. An' when I asked her if 't wasn't nice to see all the girls a-wearin' 'em—wot you think she said? 'Sickenin',' thet's wot—'sickenin'!' Now, I'm wise 'bout girls, an' I up an' tol' her she was a victim of the green-eyed monster. Then wot you think she said? 'Mittie-Maru, you needn't speak to me ever anymore.' Ruined myself pluggin' yer game along, thet's wot I did."

Thereafter whenever Chase saw one of the buttons decorating the front of a schoolgirl's blouse, he had a moment of chagrin, and called himself names for ever going into that picture gallery. And when he saw Marjory he learned what she thought of the selling of his pictures all over town for ten cents each.

"But, Marjory," said Chase, "even if they do sell so cheap it's good business. It advertises the team, and I get a percentage."

"Every girl in town can have your picture," replied Marjory severely. Evidently the possibilities of the case weighed more with Marjory than the notoriety.

Mac, too, showed concern because of the popularity of his shortstop. More than once he hinted to Chase the necessity of a ballplayer's duty not to be carried away by praise and entertainment. There would come a time, Mac averred, when he would strike a spell of bad form, when the tide of popular favor would ebb, and then he would wish he had not let himself be made so much of.

And one day toward the close of July Mac sought Chase out in the evening. He seemed eager and excited, yet anxious. He chewed on his cigar stub and talked and held to Chase.

"Got a date again tonight?" he asked for the twentieth time.

"Yes," said Chase.

"I'll let you go in a minute. There's somethin' I want to say. Chase, are you sure you won't go up in the air, if I tell you? It's great."

"What do you mean?"

"Why, I've been a little scared of all this hob-nobbin' an' fussin' of yours. You're only a kid, Chase. An' mebbe only another puff or so'll blow you out of sight."

"Haven't I listened to you always and kept both feet on the ground?"

"Sure, Chase, sure you have. I never trained a lad who took to things like you."

"You needn't worry about me, Mac. I'm having a great time here, there's no doubt about it. I like everybody. I'm not missing anything. But what they say or think about my playing hasn't anything to do with it, one way or another. On the surface it all looks easy, like real play. But you know how I've worked and am working to learn the game. I've got to succeed."

"Good! That's the spirit. Now listen. Ranney, the manager of Cincinnati, wrote me about you, an' today Burke, the manager of Detroit, was here in the grandstand watchin' your work. None of us knew it till after the game. He sneaked in foxy-like. It's jest as well, because mebbe you'd been nervous. As it was, you put up your usual hard, fast game. He sez to me jest now—I walked to the station with him—he sez, 'Thet's a fast lad; can he hit?' An' I sez, 'Can he? Well, he's been rippin' the boards off the fence all season.' Then he sez, 'Send me his battin' average, an' give me first say on him when the season's over.' "

Mac spit out his cigar, moistened his lips, and, producing papers from his pocket, went on:

"I asked Mannin' of the *Chronicle* to make out the averages. Here they are. You're hittin' .398, an' leadin' the Dude by a mile. It's hard to believe, Chase, but there's the figgers. You keep puttin' the wood on 'em, an' besides you work a good many bases on balls. Thet tells. Now get this an' keep it under your hat. If you can hang on with thet kind of stick work I'll sell you for big money when the season's over. An' if you make it an even .400 I'll give you one-third of the purchase price. Got thet!"

"Do I? Mac, I'll tear the legs off all the third basemen in the league from now on," replied Chase, with fire in his eye. He saw the tired face of his mother and her toil-worn hands, and he saw the pale, thoughtful features of his brother. That afternoon he got two triples and a home run out of five times at bat.

"Sure nothin' can stop him now!" choked Mac from the bench.

And what spoke well for Chase and his future was his popularity with the team. The "course of sprouts" had long since been gone through. Poke and Ford were now the butts of the players. Cas

adored him, Enoch called him "Sonny," now with
fatherly friendliness, the Dude and Havil sought
his society, and Benny hung to him like a leech.

"Cut out the drinking and come with me,"
Chase had said one evening. And he had taken
Benny from among the hangers-on around the
hotel, the young sports who liked to buy drinks,
the rich oilmen who had nothing but money.
Benny was ashamed and backward, but he enjoyed the evening. And Chase took him again and
came to like him.

"How much do you draw, Benny, if you don't
mind telling?" asked Chase.

"One-fifty."

"What do you do with it all?"

"Blow it in."

"Don't you save any?"

"How can a man save an' skate with thet fly
crowd? What doesn't go for booze goes for poker.
Sometimes I manage to send a ten-spot home."

"I send money home every month."

"I ought to." Benny bowed his head.

"Folks need it?"

"Lord! They're poor, sometimes awful poor when
the governor is laid up with rheumatiz. There's
Mother, she's well an' strong, but my sister's most
always ailin'. I never let myself think of them
when I'm sober, an' can't when I'm drunk."

"Benny, you'd be the best second baseman in

154

this league if you didn't drink. Think how much you could help your folks, even now, let alone what you might do if you worked up to a bigger job."

"I don't care so much for the booze. There's always somebody jollyin' me," said Benny.

It happened that Chase knew a Molly McCoy, a saucy, sparkling-eyed girl who admired Benny and wanted to meet him. So Chase, when he had worn off Benny's rough edges and made him manifest some interest in his appearance, took him to see Molly. The little lady fell in with Chase's deep-laid plot, perhaps more from the eternal feminine than from any other reason, and she made her sparkling eyes complete Chase's good beginning. She attached Benny to herself. And he, unable to comprehend, quite overcome, stuttered to Chase about it, and said most foolish and irrelevant things.

Wise Chase! He pretended there was nothing remarkable about the matter. To be sure, Molly was simply delightful. Of course she had wonderfully lovely eyes. He took care to hint to Benny that there were any number of young men in town who thought so and tried to tell Molly so. And lastly Chase said, as if it were a thing Benny did not need to be told, as if it were a simple conclusion, "It wouldn't do to drink if any fellow wanted to go with Molly."

Benny bought gorgeous neckties regularly after that, looked mysterious when his player friends chaffed him, and was cool toward his former boon companions. The hotel barrooms seldom saw him, and it was noticeable that the heated flush had faded out of his face. And when some misguided ballplayer hit a ball anywhere in the vicinity of second base the bleachers sang: "Benny's barred the door!"

During the latter half of July, Findlay kept the lead over Columbus by a small margin. And when that team presented itself for a series of three games the excitement waxed keen.

After the first game, which Findlay won, Chase met a very agreeable, smooth-faced, quiet-looking man. Chase had seen him about town somewhere, and was under the impression that Cas or Mac had said he was one of the many gamblers known in the oil belt. He talked baseball and appeared friendly, so Chase treated him civilly. The next day he met him again. They sat in the lobby of the hotel and talked awhile. It appeared the man had an engagement with Speer and was waiting for him. Sometime later Chase saw the stranger with Speer and noticed that the latter had been drinking. This occasioned Chase some surprise, because Mac expected to pitch Speer in the next game, and Mac's rules in regard to drink were stringent.

On Saturday, when Chase passed the small park near his boarding house, he encountered the agreeable gentleman sitting on one of the park benches.

"Hello, Chase. Fine hot day for the game. Sit down. I've been enjoying the shade."

Chase took a seat, more from his habit of pleasantry than from any desire to converse with the man. He was aware of a close scrutiny, but being used to that sort of thing took little heed of it.

"How about the game today?" asked the fellow.

"We'll win. We've got to have two out of three."

"Think there's any chance to win some money?"

"I never advise bets."

The gentleman adjusted his cuffs, picked a thread off his coat sleeve, and flicked the dust from his patent leather boots. Then quite casually he glanced all around the park.

"Have you seen Speer this morning?" he asked.

"No."

"Hum! I—he said he expected to see you. Mebbe he will yet."

Then he took a roll of bills from his pocket, snapped off a rubber band, and unrolled them, showing tens and twenties, rolled them up again, and snapped on the band. He was most deliberate. His next move was to hand the roll to Chase.

"Stick that in your pocket."

Chase would have been more surprised if he had not already been the recipient of so many presents; still this seemed out of all proportion. He could not imagine why a big sum of money should be handed him by a total stranger, and he said so.

"You're wise. If not, Speer will put you wise," replied the man, again adjusting his cuffs.

"Is this money for me?"

"Sure."

"What for?"

"Aren't you wise?"

"I certainly am not."

"Well, I got a chance to win a few thousand this afternoon—"

"Here, I won't try to place any money for you."

"That bundle's for you, and you'll get another like it—if I win."

"Do you mean you are going to bet on Findlay and give me this money to make me play all the harder? Because, if you do, take it back. I couldn't play any harder for ten thousand dollars."

"Not exactly. You see I'm betting on Columbus."

"Oh-h!"

Then the man shook off his slow, deliberate manner, rose to his feet, and glanced at Chase with keen, hard eyes.

"You're wise now, aren't you?"

"Not exactly," said Chase slowly.

"It's a cinch. You're going to pull off a couple of hundred. It's like finding money. I've got Speer fixed. Now all you need to do is to fall over a couple of grounders this afternoon or make a wild throw at a critical time. See!"

"You're asking me to—"

"Lay down, be off your form—"

"You're trying to buy me to throw the game?" Chase rose unsteadily.

"Hum! Call it so if you like, but—"

In blind rage Chase threw the money in the gambler's face and pushed him violently with his left hand. The gambler staggered against the bench. Then Chase swung his right arm with all the power he could summon. Gambler and bench went down together.

"You hound!" cried Chase, quivering. "I'll have you run out of town for this."

On the instant Chase wheeled and hurried down the avenue to the hotel. He went directly to Speer's room, to find the pitcher lying on his bed looking rather sick.

"Speer! What's this I hear?" demanded Chase, and he breathlessly described the proposition that had just been made him.

"Ain't it rotten of me? He bought me, Chase. But I was drunk," said Speer, in tears. "I'm sober enough now to know what a deal it was."

"Sure you were drunk!" exclaimed Chase. "But I won't rat on you, old man. You just forget it and cut out drinking with strangers after this."

Chase bolted downstairs to collide with Mac, Cas, Enoch, and Thatcher, all going in to lunch.

"Fellows, I just punched a man who tried to buy me to throw the game. Flashed a hundred on me. Tried to put it in my pocket."

"Wha-at?" roared Cas. "Where is he?"

Mac swore. "Smooth-faced guy, well dressed, big blinker in his necktie? I saw him hangin' round. What we won't do to him—"

"Come on!" roared Cas.

"Wait; get the gang!" shouted Enoch.

But the smooth-tongued, smooth-faced gentleman could not be found. Several passengers at the station testified to seeing a gentleman answering to that description—except that he had a badly swelled and discolored eye—going north along the tracks.

That night the story was town talk and Chase was a hero.

THIRTEEN

SUNDAY BALL

"SAY, sure I got somethin' to tell you Indians thet I ain't stuck on," said Mac. "The directors hev decided to play Sunday ball!"

The boys could not have made a more passionate and angry outbreak if they had heard they were to be hanged.

"Beef! Beef!" shouted Mac, red as a lobster. "Haven't I been agin it? You puff-in-front-of-the-hotel stiffs talk as if I was to blame."

"Wha-at?" roared Castorious.

"Gimme my release!" cried Benny, who had recently taken to attending a certain church. Benny never did anything by halves.

The Dude flung his bat through a window, carrying away glass and sash. All except Chase were violent in word and action, and he was too greatly surprised to move or speak.

Mac's position often assumed exasperating phases. This was one of them. He tried reason on the most choleric of his players with about as much success as if they had been brass mules.

They persisted in venting their spleen on him. Then he lost his temper.

"Flannel-mouths! Hev you all swallowed red-hot bricks? Cheese it now, cheese it! The guy that doesn't report here Sunday gets let down, an' fined besides. Got thet?"

Chase left the grounds in some distress of mind. The past four weeks had been so perfect that he had forgotten things could go wrong. Sunday ball! It had never even occurred to him. To give up his place on the team and all the bright promise of the future he could not consider for a moment. He would have to reconcile himself to the inevitable. But what would his mother say? He might keep it from her, he did not need to tell her; she would never find it out. No! The temptation lasted only a moment. He would not deceive her.

And then a further consideration weighed upon him. If he played baseball on the Sabbath in order to attain a future success, would that success be an honest one? He was afraid it would not. He had been trained to respect the Sabbath. If he kept faith with his training he must confess Sunday games were wrong. Nevertheless he could not harbor the idea of resigning his place. This made him feel he was willfully doing wrong. And he plunged into bitterness of spirit.

It was with no little curiosity that Chase went out upon the field on Sunday. The grandstand looked as usual; many familiar faces were there. The bleachers were packed, and a line of men and boys, twenty deep, extended along to the right and left of the diamond. Chase had never seen such a crowd in the grounds. Nor had he ever seen such enthusiasm.

All at once it occurred to him that here were hundreds and thousands of boys and men who worked every hour of daylight six days in the week. They were new to him, and he saw that he was as new to them. They had never seen him play. They had never before had a chance to see a ballgame in Findlay.

A question came naturally to Chase's quick mind. Had they played the game when mere tots on the commons and learned to love it, as had he? A blind man would have answered in the affirmative. They were wild and bubbling over from sheer joy. If they loved the game and had only one day to go, albeit that day was Sunday, were they doing harm? Chase could not answer that. But he knew whatever it was for them applied also to him.

Findlay won the first Sunday game. A greater and noisier crowd had never before been in attendance. Noise! the field was a howling bedlam. The boys ran like unleashed colts; the men cheered their own players, roared at their opponents, and at each other.

In his heart Chase was trying desperately hard to justify his own part in it, and because of that he saw much and found food for reflection. Well he knew the pallor of these boys; it came from the dark, sunless foundries. The hundreds of men present had a yellowish, oily look; they were the diggers and refiners, the laborers from the oil-fields. At first Chase thought their unbridled mirth, their coarse jests at the umpire, at the players, and themselves, their unremitting wild, hoarse yells, as unnatural as strident. Then suddenly a smile here, a laugh of delight there, told him all this was only natural. These men and boys had found expression for their pent-up feelings, for a short delight in contrast to the long day. This was their hour of freedom.

"Yell! That's right, yell!" muttered Chase through his teeth as he went up to bat. He felt for them, but could not quite understand. He drove one of his famous liners against the fence. "Yell for that!" he said to himself. A long screeching, swelling howl of rapture rose from the field and stands. It rang in Chase's ears as he sped around the bases, and when, after sliding into third, he stood up, he saw a sight he never forgot. The crowd was one leaping, tossing, waving, crazy mass.

With Chase, to get the track of anything was to trail it to the end. The faces and actions of that crowd made him think; their frenzied glee made

him sad, because it reminded him of his old longing for freedom, and its very violence bespoke
the bottled-up love of play. These men and boys
wanted to play, and circumstances had made it
so they could not. They loved to play. As they
had mothers, sisters, brothers, children to support, they had no time to play. As the next best
thing they loved to see someone else play. And
they had only one day—Sunday.

"It's this way," said Chase to himself. "If these
men and boys spend their Sundays at home and
in church, then Sunday ball is wrong. If they
spend it otherwise, then Sunday ball is not
wrong."

Chase was tenacious and stubborn. He found
he had loved the game as a boy because of the
play in it; now he loved it because of what it was
doing for him, because he believed in it. And he
set himself to find out what it might be doing for
others. He could not write to his mother till he
had decided the question. So he spent much of
his leisure time going the rounds of the foundries,
factories, refineries, brickyards, and he took care
to drop into all the saloons, the beer gardens, and
dance halls. Everywhere he was known and welcomed. He asked questions, he listened, and he
watched. When another Sunday had passed he
was in possession of all he needed to know. With
immeasurable reief he decided that, while he

would rather not have played Sunday ball, it was
not wrong for him to do so. He even decided he
was doing good. Thus he settled the perplexing
question forever in his own conscience. He would
tell his mother how he had arrived at his conclusion, and as for others it did not matter what they
thought.

All this time Chase had not been blind to certain indications of coolness on the part of people
who had hitherto been pleased to be courteous
and affable. And as these indications had come
solely from chance meetings in the streets, he
began to wonder how much deeper this coldness
would go, provided he sought the society of these
persons. That thought alone kept him away from
Marjory for over a week. He believed she would
understand, and still be his friend. But instinctively he feared her mother; and he had a mo-
mentary twinge when he called to mind the young
minister so welcome in the Dean household.

One evening when a party of ladies coolly
snubbed him, Chase could stand the suspense no
longer. So he presented himself at Marjory's home,
and much to his relief found her on the porch alone.

"Chase, Mama has forbidden me to see you,"
she said, with her blue eyes on him.

Chase gulped when he saw the eyes were un-
changed, still warm and bright.

"No! Oh, Marjory, it's not so bad as that?"

"Yes. But, Chase, you just give up the Sunday games, and then everything will be all right again."

"I can't do that."

"Why not? Let them play without you."

"It's no use, Marjory. Either I play on Sundays or give up the game. And it means a good deal to me. Does your mother say it's wrong?"

"She says it's awful. And Mr. Marsden held up his hand in holy horror when he heard it. He's going to work against it—stop it."

"Do you think it's so terribly wrong?"

"Oh, Chase, for you to ask me that! Don't you know it?"

"No, I don't," replied Chase stubbornly.

"Then you won't give it up?"

"No."

"Not—not even to please me?"

"I would if I could—but I can't. Marjory, please—"

"Then—good-bye."

"Oh!" cried Chase sharply. He looked at her; the long lashes were down. "You said that as if I were— Look here, Marjory Dean! I'm working for my mother. I've seen her faint when she came home at night. I've seen her hands bleed. If every day were Sunday and baseball bad—which it's not—I'd play. What do I care for Mr. Marsden? He's so dry he rattles like a beanstalk. I don't care

167

what your mother thinks. She's—I don't care—
what—what you think, either. Good-bye!"

He strode off the porch. A low, tremulous
"Chase!" did not halt him. He was bitterly hurt,
angry, and sick. He went to his room, fought out
his bad hour alone in the dark, and then came forth
feeling himself older and resigned. But he was
more determined than ever to stand by the game.

Sunday another great throng yelled itself hoarse
at the grounds, and went home in shirtsleeves,
sweaty, tired, and happy.

Chase dressed, went to dinner, and then
strolled around to the hotel. All the boys were
there lounging in familiar groups. He thought
they all seemed rather quiet and looked queerly
at him. Before he could learn what was in the air
a policeman whom he knew well stepped up reluctantly.

"Chase, I've got a warrant for you."

The blood around Chase's heart seemed to
freeze. He stared, unable to speak.

"My pardner has gone to arrest Mac," continued the officer. "Here's the warrant." The printed
words blurred in Chase's sight, but his own name
in writing, and the term "Sunday baseball," and
the Rev. Mr. Marsden's name told him the meaning of the arrest.

"I'm sorry, Chase. I hate to run you in. But

I've my duty," said the officer, and whispered lower, "We'll try to get word to Mayor Duff, so you can get bail and not be locked up."

"Bail? Locked up?" echoed Chase, stupidly.

Mac appeared with another officer. The little manager was pale but composed.

"Sure, we're pinched, Chase," he said, and as the players crowded round he continued. "Fade away now, or you'll put people wise. Somebody hunt up King an' Beekman an' send them to the station. Cas, you dig for Mayor Duff's house an' ask him to come to take bail for us. Lord! I hope he's home. If not, the law puts us in a cell tonight. Sure somebody has done us dirt. Them warrants might have been made out for tomorrow."

"Mac, you an' Chase walk around to the station alone," said one of the officers. "We'll go another way."

"Thanks, sure you're all right," replied Mac. "Come on, Chase. Don't look so peaked."

"Isn't the whole team arrested?" queried Chase.

"Sure, an' the whole team'll be on trial, but the warrants read for manager and one player. It'd been more regular to hev pinched Enoch, as he is captain. Don't know why they picked out you."

"Is playing on Sunday against the law?"

"Naw. Not any more 'n drivin' a team; but these moss-backed people twist things an' call us 'nuis-

ances' an' 'immoral' an' Lord knows what. Here
we are at the station. It's pretty tough on you,
kid, but don't quit. This won't hurt you any."

The two officers met them, unlocked the sta-
tionhouse doors, and ushered them into the may-
or's office. Presently Beekman strode in, big and
important, and said it was not necessary to call in
King, for he would go bail for both.

"If Duff's in town he'll come," continued Beekman.

Presently the sounds of a fast-trotting horse and
flying wheels drew an officer to the window.

"The mayor's here," he said.

Mac settled back with a deep breath. "Good!"
he exclaimed.

A tall man with a gray beard came in hurriedly,
followed by Castorious. He nodded to all, threw
his gloves on the desk, and took the warrants held
out to him. In a few moments he had made the
necessary recording of the arrests and of accepted
bail. Then he shook hands with Mac and Chase.

"Glad I happened to run across Castorious. Was
driving out into the country. You'll get your hearing tomorrow morning, and if you wish I'll set the
trial for Wednesday or Thursday morning."

"The sooner the better," replied Mac.

Then the mayor bowed pleasantly and left.
Chase followed the others out. He could scarcely
realize that he had been arrested; and, leaving

his friends in earnest conversation, he went to his room and to bed. He did not have a very restful night.

The morning papers were full of the particulars of the arrest and the consideration of Sunday ball; and the subject was the absorbing topic of conversation everywhere. All the directors of the team were present at the hearing, and afterward repaired to Judge Meggs's office to discuss the matter of defense.

Meggs was a shrewd old lawyer, and incidentally an admirer of the game of baseball. While in office he had been known to adjourn court because he wanted to see Findlay "wallop" their rivals. Therefore it was felt that with the case in his hands the team would escape imprisonment and fine even if Sunday ball were discontinued.

Beekman and King had visited practically all the men of business in Findlay, and stating their case, that the Sunday game was conducted in an orderly manner, that no drinks were sold at or near the grounds, that it was played at the earnest request of thousands of working men and boys, had gotten a long list of signatures to their petition favoring the game.

During the discussion as to the defense one of the directors had mentioned the fact that certain members of the laboring class were better off in summer for the playing of the game.

"Can we prove that?" asked Judge Meggs.

"I know it's true," spoke up Chase.

"How do you know?" returned the lawyer.

Somewhat incoherently, but with the eager earnestness of conviction, Chase told what he knew. Then the judge questioned him in regard to his motive, drew him out to tell what baseball meant to him and to others like him, with the result that he presently said to the directors:

"Gentlemen, we have our defense, and you may take my word for it, we shall win."

He asked Chase to call at his office an hour before the time fixed upon for the trial the next day.

Findlay lost the ballgame that afternoon. They played listlessly and plainly showed the effects of the cloud hanging over them.

On Wednesday Chase went to Judge Meggs's office at the appointed time.

"Now, Chase, if you are a star of the diamond you ought to shine just as brightly in the court-room. This morning when I call on you I want you to get up and tell the court what you told me about yourself and baseball. Be simple, earnest, and straightforward. You have here the oppor-tunity to vindicate yourself and your fellow play-ers, so make the best of it."

Chase went to the courtroom with the judge. It was crowded with people. The Findlay team and the team visiting town at that time occupied front seats. All the directors and many business-men were present. There was a plentiful sprin-kling of ladies in the background.

Mayor Duff opened proceedings as soon as the judge arrived with Chase.

The prosecuting minister did not appear. His representative, a young lawyer, rose and expa-tiated on the evils of the Findlay team in general and of Sunday ball in particular.

These young men set bad examples, engen-dered idleness and love of play, they were op-posed to work, they enticed boys from school to see a useless and sometimes dangerous sport, they fostered the spirit of rivalry, of gambling.

Baseball on Sunday was an abomination, it was a desecration of the Sabbath, it added to the un-dermining of the church, it opposed the teachings of the Bible, it kept the boys and girls from Sun-day school. Sunday was a day of rest, of prayer, of quiet communion, not a day for playing, howl-ing, yelling, mobbing, carousing. The permitting of the game was a disgrace to the decent name of Findlay, a shame to her respectable citizens, and a sin to her churches.

The prosecution examined witnesses, who swore to endless streams of passing men on the streets; of yelling that made the afternoon a hid-eous nightmare; of brawls on corners and mob violence in the ballgrounds; of hoodlums accosting women. And there the prosecution rested.

Judge Meggs read the petition and the names of the men who had signed it; and he said there could be little doubt of the great benefit Findlay had derived in a business way from the advertising given to it by the baseball team.

"Your Honor," he concluded, impressively, "I will now have one of the defendants tell of his experience of baseball."

At a word from Judge Meggs, Chase stepped forward. His face was white, his eyes dark from excitement, but he appeared entirely self-possessed.

"Your Honor, I am eighteen years old, and have played baseball as long as I can remember. I learned in the streets and on the lots of Akron. When twelve years old I left school to work to support my mother and a crippled brother. I sold papers, did odd jobs, anything that was offered. I had a crooked eye then, and it was hard for me to get a place. People didn't like my looks. At fourteen I went to work in the molding department of a factory. I studied at night to try to get some education. When I had been there a year I earned five dollars a week. After four years I was earning six dollars. I did not advance fast.

"Last summer I played ball on the factory team. This spring I decided to be a ballplayer. My mother opposed me, but I persuaded her. I started out to find a place on a team. My crooked eye worked against my chances of success. I became a tramp, and beat my way from town to town. I starved—but I hung on.

"One morning I awoke in a fence corner. A woman I spoke to said the town nearby was Findlay. I hunted up the ballgrounds and the manager. He didn't see my ragged clothes or my crooked eye. He gave me a chance. I played a wretched game. I expected to be thrown from the grounds. He gave me money, said he would keep me, would teach me the game. I tried hard and I made good.

"I have been very happy here in Findlay. I never knew what friends meant. Everybody has been kind to me. I have dreamed of one day being a businessman here. But best for me was what I could do for my mother and brother. She does not take in washing anymore or sew herself blind late into the nights. My brother has had treatment for his hip; he has the books he needed, and he will get the education he longs for.

"When I learned we were to play Sunday ball I was stunned. I never thought of that. My mother gave me Christian teaching, and I kept the Sabbath day. I was sick with doubt. I felt that I was going to do wrong. I concluded that it would be wrong, but I had no mind to sacrifice my place on the team. That had been too dearly bought. It meant too much to me.

175

"My mother had to be told, and there lay the reason of my seeking for some excuse. It came to me in the first Sunday game. There were five hundred men and boys who had never attended one of our games. No one ever saw a wilder crowd. It was as if they had been let out of an asylum. They were crazy, but it was with happiness. They screamed like Indians, but it was for freedom. I saw men smash their hats, boys throw their coats; and boys yell with tears in their eyes. Why?

"Your Honor, I will tell you why. I know what it means to work from daylight to night, year in, year out, with no chance, no hope for the natural play every man and especially every boy loves. It is very easy for ministers and teachers to tell us working men how to spend the one free day, and no doubt they mean well, but they miss the point. On Sunday those shrieking, boisterous diggers, cappers, puddlers, refiners, had gone back to their boyhood. They played the game for us with their hearts, their throats, their tears.

"The night after that game I had a change of feeling. I began to think perhaps after all it was not so bad for me to play ball on Sunday. I began to see things I had never seen before. If I could satisfy myself that the hundreds of men and boys were better off at a Sunday game than elsewhere, then I was justified in playing for their amusement.

"So I began to go around and ask questions. At first this searching for the truth was because of what I must tell my mother; afterward the thing itself interested me. I went to the foundries and factories, to the big refineries, to the brickyards—everywhere. And I found everybody knew me; everybody had a word for me; everybody's eyes shone at the mention of the next Sunday game. I talked to little boys and girls carrying dinner to their fathers, and I went home with them and talked to their mothers. One and all, these mothers welcomed the game.

"I visited the saloons and beer gardens, the road houses and the dance halls. I found them bitterly opposed to Sunday ball. Their Sunday business was ruined. Two big gardens closed up after the second Sunday. I had seen some of these places when in full blast on a busy Sunday. The beer ran in streams and the air reeked.

"It seems to me that those who make the laws would learn something if they would become mere hard-working men. When their eyes burned in their heads, and their backs ached, and they never saw the sky, and grew dull and weary, they would see differently. They wouldn't ask any man to sit in church and be told how to be good and happy. A man or a boy penned up all the week needs some kind of a fling. Your Honor, I wrote my mother that I was not doing wrong when I played Sunday ball. I am not ashamed of it. We players are not a disgrace to Findlay."

Chase sat down. Judge Meggs stroked his chin and watched His Honor, while the crowd roared their applause. Finally Mayor Duff rapped on his desk.

"I am sitting in judgment on this case as mayor of Findlay, as a deacon of the church bringing the action, and as a director of the Findlay Baseball Association. I am rather submerged in the deep sea between the two sides. But I am happy to say that as mayor, church member, and director I have solved the problem.

"I do not want to go on record as agreeing entirely with Alloway; still, so far as he is concerned, I uphold him. More than that, he has given us something to think about. I have long had my eye on those halls and gardens he spoke of and now they shall be closed on Sundays.

"During the last few days I have visited every prominent business concern in Findlay, and I have laid before each this baseball situation. In substance, I said I would permit Sunday ball unless they gave their employees a half holiday on Saturdays. I have spoken of Findlay's prosperity, and that no small factor in the activity of business for the last few years has been the advertisement of our crack baseball team. I have gone to the different leaders of the churches and of society, thing you see is pea-green."

lted? Perfeckly rude, ain't I?
me sense into yer block. You
, an' I wanter put in my oar.
u know, you'll be hevin' a
ecord'll go to ballyhoo. Lis-
liss Marjory most every day
away, an' I hed my troubles
u ain't finished with to Miss

t, turning wildly to Mittie,

y?"
e to. Sorry! Say, Marjory's
blue out'en her eyes cryin'.
vhen she's with me, so thet's
ck, as usual."
ie—s-say?"
ch 'cept, 'Mittie, he's angry
with me? Will he stay angry
he weeps some more."
d Chase.
've any regard fer my friend-
An' yer wrong about Miss
gel. She's a little devil. I tell
; the fire fly fer thet bunch
. She won't go to church or
sore at her mother an' won't

and I have solicited their cooperation, assuring them if they would join forces with me for the good of Findlay and the laboring classes and the baseball people, there need be no Sunday ball.

"I am happy to say that I have been entirely successful. There will be no Sunday ball. There will be no open shops or factories or mills on Saturday afternoons. We, all of us, working people, church people, everybody concerned, will profit by this. How much better it is for the baseball team to have the undivided support of Findlay! That is what it will now have. Findlay is proud of its baseball team. And it is proud of some other things—its prosperity, its good name, its old-fashioned institutions. We want still to have the quiet, serene Sundays our fathers and mothers had.

"I think it is to the credit of Findlay that we can meet this question and settle it to everybody's satisfaction. I am sure the matter has been wholesome for us as a city and as individuals.

"So I am happy to dismiss the case, assuring the prosecution and the defense that they both have won, and that their victory is in every way an advance, a betterment, for the commonwealth of Findlay."

WAITING IT OUT

IT was a good thing for Chase and his batting average that, right after the trial, the Findlay team took their usual monthly trip on the road. Chase's hitting had been slowly dropping off, except for an occasional vicious double or triple during the last two weeks; but once away from home he returned rapidly to form. The team broke even on the trip, a satisfactory showing to Mac. "Sure, we're restin' up fer the break into the stretch," he said.

They came home to find the town more stirred up than ever. The faction that had opposed the game now printed editorials, sent circulars and petitions, preached sermons, and worked indefatigably for Mac and his players, and therefore created all the more interest. The directors came out with an announcement that, owing to the increased patronage, it was necessary to have more seating capacity, and they erected another open stand.

Chase was all the more popular, and more

down, an' now eve

"Mittie-Maru—'

"Go wan! Yer ins
Say, I wanter beat s
can't fool me. I kno
See! Fust thing y
slump, an' yer fine
ten, I've been with
while the team was
cheerin' her up. Yo
Marjory at all!"

Chase gave a sta
and stuttered,

"Is-s-s—she s-sor

"Tho't you'd con
washed all the sky-
She can't cry except
how I git it in the n

"Wh-what—did s

"She don't say m
with me. Is he angry
with me?' An' then

"Angel!" murmur

"Say, Chase, if yo
ship—cut thet out!
Marjory's bein' an a
you, I bet she make
as was after yer scal
Sunday school. She'

and I have solicited their cooperation, assuring them if they would join forces with me for the good of Findlay and the laboring classes and the baseball people, there need be no Sunday ball.

"I am happy to say that I have been entirely successful. There will be no Sunday ball. There will be no open shops or factories or mills on Saturday afternoons. We, all of us, working people, church people, everybody concerned, will profit by this. How much better it is for the baseball team to have the undivided support of Findlay! That is what it will now have. Findlay is proud of its baseball team. And it is proud of some other things—its prosperity, its good name, its old-fashioned institutions. We want still to have the quiet, serene Sundays our fathers and mothers had.

"I think it is to the credit of Findlay that we can meet this question and settle it to everybody's satisfaction. I am sure the matter has been wholesome for us as a city and as individuals.

"So I am happy to dismiss the case, assuring the prosecution and the defense that they both have won, and that their victory is in every way an advance, a betterment, for the commonwealth of Findlay."

WAITING IT OUT

IT was a good thing for Chase and his batting average that, right after the trial, the Findlay team took their usual monthly trip on the road. Chase's hitting had been slowly dropping off, except for an occasional vicious double or triple during the last two weeks; but once away from home he returned rapidly to form. The team broke even on the trip, a satisfactory showing to Mac. "Sure, we're restin' up fer the break into the stretch," he said.

They came home to find the town more stirred up than ever. The faction that had opposed the game now printed editorials, sent circulars and petitions, preached sermons, and worked indefatigably for Mac and his players, and therefore created all the more interest. The directors came out with an announcement that, owing to the increased patronage, it was necessary to have more seating capacity, and they erected another open stand.

Chase was all the more popular, and more

sought-after than ever, but he could not take the
pleasure in it that he had derived before his arrest.
He was quiet and preoccupied, and haunted the
ballgrounds on mornings and practiced batting till
Mac drove him out. "You Indian, you'll go stale!"
cried Mac. "Besides, you're battin' all my practice
balls over the fence for the kids to steal."

Chase thought that a thousand persons beaming
upon him could not make up for the coldly averted
look of one individual. He fondly imagined that
the few whom he met at long intervals, who
passed him by as if he were nothing, were the
occasion of his gloom. He began to revel in a
species of self-pity. It remained for him to learn
a good deal from his staunch friend, Mittie-Maru.

"Down in the mouth agin? Didn't I onct hear
you ask Mac, 'Wot you want fer fifteen cents—
canary birds?' Chase, me old college chum,
you've got the pip. You couldn't see tru a mill-
stone wid a hole in it. Ain't you *it* round these
diggin's? Sure as yer born, one of the big teams'll
cop you out this fall. Thet'll mean two t'ousand
next season. An' here you go mopin' round like a
dead one. Wot's the matter wid you?"

"I'm just a little off my feed, Mittie, I guess."

"I reckon it's not thet. You've got the dingest
case I ever seen, Chase. A pair of sky-blue eyes
hev been yer finish. It's a case of shutout! No-hit
game! Not a look in! Marjory's folks hev turn you

down, an' now everything you see is pea-green."

"Mittie-Maru—"

"Go wan! Yer insulted? Perfeckly rude, ain't I? Say, I wanter beat some sense into yer block. You can't fool me. I know, an' I wanter put in my oar. See! Fust thing you know, you'll be hevin' a slump, an' yer fine record'll go to ballyhoo. Listen, I've been with Miss Marjory most every day while the team was away, an' I hed my troubles cheerin' her up. You ain't finished with to Miss Marjory at all!"

Chase gave a start, turning wildly to Mittie, and stuttered,

"Is-s-s—she s-sorry?"

"Tho't you'd come to. Sorry! Say, Marjory's washed all the sky-blue out'en her eyes cryin'. She can't cry except when she's with me, so thet's how I git it in the neck, as usual."

"Wh-what—did she—s-say?"

"She don't say much 'cept, 'Mittie, he's angry with me. Is he angry with me? Will he stay angry with me?' An' then she weeps some more."

"Angel!" murmured Chase.

"Say, Chase, if you've any regard fer my friendship—cut thet out! An' yer wrong about Miss Marjory's bein' an angel. She's a little devil. I tell you, I bet she makes the fire fly fer thet bunch as was after yer scalp. She won't go to church or Sunday school. She's sore at her mother an' won't

is. Cas finally got hold of Algy, and it surely was time enough!"

"There's always something new and funny at a ballgame," said the judge with his hearty laugh. "Now, Chase, let's talk business. I've got a proposition to make to you. Have you planned anything for the winter?"

"No."

"Is there any reason why you could not have your mother and brother come to live in Findlay?"

"Why, I guess not."

"I'm glad to hear it. I've got a job for you, seventy-five a month to start with. Meggs and Company—you know my brother's big store, groceries, wholesale and retail, hardware, oilmen's supplies, etc. I'm a member of the firm. We are investing heavily in new oilfields—branching out. You'll be busy in the store and keeping track of the men. You'll have a chance to learn things. This job will be ready for you soon. In the meantime you can hang around in the mornings and get on to your work. How does the idea strike you?"

"Thank you—why—it's simply bully. Only— does that mean I must give up baseball?"

"Certainly not. It's a winter's work for you. You must stick to baseball till you've made some money. But I take it you won't loaf between seasons. I just thought I'd throw this in your way. We need a young man. And as I hinted, there might turn up something of future value to you."

"I accept—thank you very much."

"Now here's another idea. There's a cottage and a plot of ground, ten acres, I think, on Elm Street, just on the outskirts of town. It's a pretty place and for sale cheap. A little money on repairs would make it a nice home. There's an orchard, a grove of maples, and the river runs along the edge of it. This place would be a good investment at twice the price asked for it. I know. I am interested in a real-estate deal with some men here. King's one, so's Mayor Duff. We're going to develop a good bit of ground to the north of town. Prices will go up out that way. I can get this place on any terms you want. You can buy it for less than rent. You run out there the first thing tomorrow, and if you like the place, come to my office, and we'll close the deal. Now let's have a game of billiards."

Chase left the judge and went to his room with his mind too full of plans to permit him to sleep till late in the night. He awakened early, and, breakfast being entirely superfluous, he hurried north to Elm Street and thence to the outskirts of town.

There was no mistaking the cottage, because it was the only one. Chase felt it was altogether out of the question for him to own such a place. The cottage sat back from the road on a little hill. It was low, many-gabled, vine-covered, and had a porch all the way around. A giant maple shaded the western side. Chase went in. The first room was long, had a deep seat in a bay window and an open fireplace. He saw in fancy a fire blazing there on a winter's evening. There was a dining room and kitchen, and a cozy pantry. Upstairs were four bedrooms. The west one, all bay windows and bright, would be for his mother; the adjoining one would be Will's; and a little room in the back, from which he saw the grove and the river, would be his. Then he punched himself and said, "I'm dreaming again."

He looked into the well in the backyard and straightway began singing "The Old Oaken Bucket." He flew through the orchard and ran into the grove of maples. The trees, the fence, the hill sloped down to the river. There was a little fall and a deep pool and a great mossy stone.

"I've got to hurry back to the judge's and be waked out of this," muttered Chase, "What would Mittie think? He'd say there'd never be any hope of my coming down after this ascension."

Chase started for town. He would run a little way, then check himself, only to break out into another dash. He got to Judge Meggs's office before opening hours and sat down to wait. The time dragged. One moment he would call himself a fool and the next he remembered the judge's kindly eyes.

"Well, well, good morning, Chase. The early bird catches the worm. Come in, come in. And how'd you like the cottage?"

Chase stuttered and broke out into unintelligible speech. Then he grew more confused and bewildered. He heard the kind voice and felt the kind hand on his shoulder. He remembered running breathlessly to the bank and drawing a sum of money. He signed his name to stamped papers. And then the judge was telling him that the property was his.

Chase finished this wonderful morning of mornings in his room. After a long time he got a logical idea of things. He had bought the property for eighteen hundred dollars, two hundred down and twenty each month until the debt was canceled. The deeds were signed and stamped. And most strange and remarkable of all was to read the name of the former owner—Silas Meggs.

Chase spent another morning consulting carpenters, plasterers, paper hangers; and the next he presented himself at the store of Meggs and Company. He was told to spend his time for the present in the different oilfields, familiarizing himself with men, conditions, and machinery. And the senior member of the firm added significantly: "You need not mention your connection with us for a while yet. Just be looking round casually. But be sharp as a steel trap. You may learn things of interest to us."

Chase wondered what next would happen to him. There was certainly a thrill in the prospect before him. Such men as Judge Meggs and his brother would not stoop to the employing of a spy, but they might well have use for a detective. Chase had heard strange stories from the oilfields.

The oil belt was a scene of great activity that summer. Strikes, unprecedented in the history of boring wells, had been made. All over the belt rose a forest of wooden derricks, with their ladders, and queer wheels, and enormous pump handles ceaselessly working up and down. Pipes ran in all directions; huge tanks loomed up everywhere; puffs of smoke marked the pumping engines sheltered in little huts; the ground was black and oily, and the smell of oil was overpowering.

"Crude oil seventy cents a barrel!" ejaculated Chase, as he watched the great comical-looking handles bobbing up, some of them pumping a hundred barrels a day. "These oilmen get rich while they sleep!"

Chase found that as he was known in the factories and brickyards, so was he known in the oilfields. All gates opened to him. Every grimy workman found time to stop and have a word with him. The governor of Ohio could not have com-

manded the interest, to say nothing of the friendliness, accorded to the boy baseball player. It was
not long before Chase appreciated his usefulness
to Meggs and Company. He had a pleasant word
for every worker. "Hello! I'm out looking over the
oilfield. Say! That's interesting work of yours. Tell
me about it."

Then a grimy face would break into a smile.
"Howdy, Chase. I were jest thinkin' about the
team. Close race, ain't it? But we'll put it all over
Columbus next week. I'll be there Saturday an'
hope you knock the socks off one. Work, this's
rotten work I'm on here. Don't need to be done
at all." And the baseball fan would tell the baseball
player details of work that a superintendent could
not have dragged from him. Every engineer and
prospector and driller cared to rest and talk to
Chase. The boy was bright and pleasant; but the
magic halo of a ballplayer's fame was the secret
of his reception. So it was that he learned things,
and surprised the senior member, and won an
approving word from the judge.

Chase did not visit the same part of the oilfields
twice. The wide belt extended a hundred miles
toward Lima and beyond; it would have required
months to go over it all. One morning he went
out to see a new well, called "The Geyser," just
struck, and reported to be the biggest well in the
fields. He found a scene of great excitement. Em-

bankments had been thrown up three feet all around the well to catch the jet of oil. There was a lake of oil three feet deep; in some places it broke over the embankment.

With more than his usual luck he met an Irishman who had come to him during one of the games and tried to give him part of a wager he had won on Findlay.

"Hello, Pat. Somebody's struck a dandy, eh?"

"Sure it's the ould man hisself. Coom round, let me show you. He blowed the bloomin' derrick a mile, but we got him under control now."

"Who are the owners?"

"Dean and Pitman Company," replied Pat.

Chase pricked up his ears. He knew that this Dean was Marjory's father. He had learned the firm was in a bad financial strait, having repeatedly backed unproductive ventures. When he saw the lake of oil he had a warm glow of pleasure; he was glad for Marjory's sake.

"What's the flow? Must be a regular river."

"Flow? He'll flow a hundred thousand barrels a day fer a while, an' thet without a pump."

"Whew!" exlaimed Chase.

"It's tu bad, tu bad! Sich a grand well!" said Pat. "But he'll niver last."

"Why not?"

Pat winked mysteriously, but offered no explanation. Chase left him and talked with the other men. He found that the land on which the well had been struck belonged to Findlay farmers, and a lease of it had been sought by one of the greatest oil companies in the world. Chase's next move was to find out from the farmers thereabouts if there was any unleased land adjoining. There was one plot of ground, hilly, rocky, unpractical for boring, that stood close to the field of "The Geyser," and which had just been leased by a large company. Chase strolled over the field and to his great surprise was ordered off. Then a man evidently in authority recognized Chase and countermanded the order, giving as excuse some trifling remark about thieves. Chase did not believe the man. He sauntered round, as if he were killing time, talked baseball with the men, and remained only a short while.

But once out of sight he started to run, and he never stopped till he reached the trolley line. He boarded a car, rode into town, leaped off, and again began running. At the office of Dean & Pitman a boy said Mr. Pitman was out of town and Mr. Dean at lunch. Then Chase once again took to his heels.

Breathlessly he dashed upon the porch and knocked on the door of the Dean house. Marjory opened it and uttered a cry at sight of Chase.

"Where's—your—father?" he demanded.

Marjory turned white and began to tremble. The blue eyes widened.

"P-Papa—is—is at lunch. Oh—Chase!"

"Tell him I want to see him quick—quick!"

His sharp voice rang clearly through the house. A chair scraped and hurried steps preceded the appearance of Mr. Dean, a little weather-beaten man of mild aspect.

"What's this?"

"Mr. Dean, I've been out to the oilwell. The field next to yours has been leased by the Monarch Company. They are drilling day and night, and they know they can't strike oil there. It's a plot to ruin 'The Geyser.' They'll sink a thousand pounds of dynamite, explode it, and forever ruin your well. Come on. You haven't much time. They're nearly ready. I saw everything. It's a cold fact. But you can hold them up. We'll get Wilson, the expert, and an officer, and stop the work. Come on! Come on!"

FIFTEEN

THE GREAT GAME

ON the third day of the last series between Columbus and Findlay, the percentage of games won favored the former team by several points. If Columbus won the deciding game, which was the last on their schedule, they would win the pennant. If Findlay won, the percentage would go to a tie; but having three more games with the tail-end Mansfield team they were practically sure of capturing the flag.

The excitement in and about Findlay was intense. Stores and shops and fields closed before noon that Saturday. The pride of Findlay rose in arms. Class was forgotten in loyalty to the common cause.

The Pastime Ballpark opened at one o'clock and closed its gates at two-thirty, packed to its utmost capacity. Hundreds of people were left clamoring outside.

The grandstand made a brave picture. Quality was out in force today. The mass of white and blue of the ladies, and their bright moving fans and soft murmuring laughter, lent the scene that last charm which made it softly gay.

Out on the bleachers and in the roped-off sidelines was a dense, hilarious, coatless, and vestless mob. Peanuts flew like hail in a storm. From one end of the grounds to the other passed a long ripple of unrestrained happiness. The sky shone blue, the field gleamed green, the hour of play was at hand.

The practice of both teams received more applause than average games; and the batting order, at last posted on the huge blackboard, elicited an extra roar.

FINDLAY		COLUMBUS	
Winters	3B	Welch	LF
Thatcher	CF	Kelly	SS
Chase	SS	Horn	C
Havil	LF	Wilson	3B
Benny	2B	Harvey	CF
Ford	1B	O'Rourke	RF
Speer	RF	Starke	2B
Hicks	C	Hains	1B
Castorious	P	Ward	P

Umpire, O'Connor

Mac threw up his hands when he saw the name of the umpire. The truth of the matter was that Mac was in a highly nervous state. Managing a ballteam was only one point less trying than governing an army in the field. The long campaign had worn Mac out.

"Silk!" he exclaimed. "I wired the president to send any umpire but Silk. He's after us!"

Then Cas put on Algy's coat of white and blue and sent him out. Algy knew his business. As the gong called the Columbus players in from practice, Algy pranced around the diamond. When he reached the plate Cas, who had stepped from the bench, called sharply to him. Algy promptly stood up on his hind legs.

"That's for Findlay!" yelled Cas to the stands.

Then Algy made a ludicrous but valiant effort to stand on his head.

"That's for Columbus!" yelled Cas.

The long laughing roar of the delighted crowd attested to the popular regard for the great pitcher and his dog.

"What'll we take, the field or bat?" asked Mac, beginning to fidget.

"Hev you lost your head?" enquired Enoch softly. "Bat! the bat! Now, fellers, git in the game. We're all on edge. Ward has always been hard for us to beat, but if we can once git him started it's all off."

"Chase, come here," said Mac; then he whispered, "I can't keep it. Burke, the Detroit manager, is up in the stands. For Lord's sake, break loose today. Mannin' sez to me jest a minute ago thet if you git two hits in this game your average'll go over .400. I oughtn't to tell you, but I can't help it."

"I'm glad you did," replied Chase, with his fingers clenching into his bat.

"Ward's got steam today," growled Mittie-Maru. "You guys want 'er perk up!"

"Play ball!" called Silk.

The crowd shouted one quick welcoming cry and then subsided into watchful waiting suspense.

Enoch hit a fly to Kelly, and Thatcher went out, Wilson to Hains. Chase sent a slow grounder toward short. Wilson fielded the ball as quickly as possible and made a good throw, but Chase, running like a deer, beat the ball to first. The eager crowd opened up. Havil, however, fell a victim to Ward's curves.

For Columbus Welch hit safely, Kelly sacrificed, sending the fleet left fielder to second. On the next play he stole third and scored on Horn's long fly to Havil. Wilson fouled out.

Findlay 0, Columbus 1.

Mac began to fidget worse than ever and greeted Cas with a long face.

"Wot's the matter with you? Ball doesn't seem to hev any speed."

Cas deigned not to notice the little manager.

When Benny got a base on balls Mac nudged the player next to him and brightened up. "Bunt,

Ford," he said, and when Ford laid down a neat sacrifice Mac nudged the player on the other side. "Thet's good; thet's good!" Speer hit safely, scoring Benny. Thereupon Mac jammed his elbow into Enoch's ribs and bubbled over.

"Makin' sausage agin, hey?" enquired the genial captain with soft sarcasm.

All the players had sore ribs from these jabs of Mac's elbows. He had the most singular way, when the team was winning, of slipping from one end of the bench to the other, jabbing his appreciation of good plays into the anatomy of his long-suffering team. Cas never sat on the bench and Enoch, always forgetful, usually came in for most of the jabs.

Hicks made a good bid for a hit, but, being slow, could not get to first ahead of the ball. Speer went to third. Cas got a double along the left foul line, Enoch walked on balls, and Thatcher's hit scored Cas. The Columbus second baseman caught Enoch trying to get a lead off second.

Findlay 3, Columbus 1.

All the while the crowd roared, and all the while Mac on the bench was going through his peculiar evolutions. "A bingo! Good!"—jab and jab—"Will you look at thet?"—jab and jab—"Keep after 'em"—jab and jab—"Oh! Oh! run, you Indian, run."—jab, jab, jab.

Neither team scored in the third; Findlay failed

again in the fourth, but Columbus tied the score. The game began to get warm.

With one man out Chase opened the fifth with a hard hit to right. He believed he could stretch it into a double and strained every nerve. He saw the second baseman brace himself, and without slackening his speed he leaped feetfirst into the air. He struck the ground and shot through the dust to the base. Just an instant after, he felt the baseman tag him sharply with the ball. Lying there, Chase looked for the umpire. Silk came racing down, swept his right hand toward the sidelines, and said,

"You made a grand slide—but you're out!"

It seemed then that Chase's every vein burst with the mad riot of hot blood. He sprang to his feet. "Out! Out! Why, he never touched me till after I hit the bag."

"Don't show off before Burke," called Silk. "You're out! Perambulate!"

Chase stamped in his fury, but the mention of Burke cooled him. As he walked off, the whole Findlay team, led by Mac, made for the umpire with angry eyes.

"Go back! Go back!" yelled Silk. "To the bench! I'm running this game. To the bench or I'll flash my watch!"

The uproar in the stands and bleachers gave place to an uproar back of center field. A portion of fence suddenly crashed forward, and through the gap poured a black stream of yelling boys and men.

That one bad decision had served to upset Mac's equilibrium, and he was now raging. Enoch reasoned with him, Cas swore at him, some of the other players gave him sharp answers. Mac was plainly not himself. He showed it in that inning when he discarded the usual signs and told the team to go ahead on its own hook. Havil and Benny failed to get on base, and once more the Columbus team trotted in to bat.

Then the unexpected, the terrible, happened. By sharp hitting Columbus scored five runs. Cas labored in the box, but he could not stem the torrent of basehits. A fast double play by Chase and Benny and a good catch by Havil retired the side.

Findlay 3, Columbus 8.

A profound gloom settled over the field. The bleachers groaned and a murmur ran through the grandstand. Cas walked up to the bench and confronted Mac.

"I'm done," said the great pitcher, simply. "My speed's gone. I strained my arm the last game. You'd better put Poke in. He's left-handed, and his speed will likely fool Columbus after my floaters. But say, I won't go out till I get a chance to get after Silk. He needs a little jacking up. He wouldn't give me the corners. I'll make him sick. And, fellows, don't quit."

"Oh! We're licked! We're licked!" cried Mac. Anyone to have seen his face would have known how hard he had worked and what the pennant meant to him. But his players evidently were not of the same mind. They were mostly silent with knitted brows and compressed lips. Mittie-Maru never wavered in his crisp, curt encouragement.

"Wot t' 'll! Wot do we care fer five runs? A couple of bingos an' Ward's in the air. We kin win with two out in the ninth, an' here we got enough time left to win two games. Stick at 'em! Don't quit! Keep the yellow down! We'll put this game on ice, all right, all right!"

Cas slowly walked up to the plate. The great crowd had not hope enough to cheer. When the umpire called the first ball, which was pretty well up to Cas's chin, a strike, the crowd yelled. Cas turned square round and glared long at Silk. That worthy called another strike while Cas's back was turned to the pitcher. He did right, of course, but the crowd did not know it or think so. And they yelled louder. Cas made no effort to hit at the next ball, which also was a strike.

"Out!" called Silk, adjusting his indicator.

Cas turned upon the umpire. No tragedian ever put forth a greater effect of outraged scorn and injustice.

"Wha-at?" he roared in a voice that penetrated to the remotest corners of the field.

"Three strikes and out!" repeated Silk.

"It was wide," yelled Cas grandly.

"Batter up," called Silk.

"Say, haven't I a right to speak a word?" demanded Cas. He deliberately walked up to Silk. It was Cas's ruse, a trick as old as baseball, to make a fierce stand in order to influence the umpire on future close decisions. Poor umpires! Theirs was the thankless task, the difficult task, and they were only human.

"You're way off today, Silk," went on Cas. "You're rotten. You wouldn't give me the corners, but you give them to Ward."

"Back to the bench," ordered Silk.

"Can't I say a word?"

"Not to me."

"You're rotten!"

"Costs you twenty-five!"

"Ha! Now you're going some! Threw off my pitching, struck me out, and now you fine me. We've got a grand show with you calling the plays. Make it fifty, you robber!"

"Fifty it is!" replied Silk.

"Put me out of the game! You're from Columbus! Go ahead! Put me out of the game!"

"Out you go!" shouted Silk.

The crowd heard and rose with a roar of rage.

Cas was their idol, and they were with him to a man. They stamped, yelled, and hissed their disapproval. It began to be a tight place for Silk, and he knew it. Right was on his side but under trying circumstances such as these, right did not always triumph.

"Put me off the grounds!" bawled Cas.

"Off you go!" yelled Silk, white in the face.

Then Cas showed his understanding of the crowd and the serious nature of the situation. He had turned his trick; now to avert real disaster. It would not have been wise for an umpire to call the game in the face of that angry grandstand and crazy bleachers. Not one umpire in a hundred would have had the nerve. But it was evident that Cas thought Silk might, for he was not afraid of anything. So Cas waved his long arms to the crowds, motioning for them to sit down.

"All right, Silk, out for me." Cas ran for the bench and grabbed his sweater. He shook his big fist in Poke's face. "Now, Rube, at 'em! Fast and straight over the pan! Mittie, you roast this bunch of deaders back to life."

Mac was sitting with his head bowed in his hands. At Cas's last words he raised a heartbroken face, and began to rail at the umpire, at Cas for having a glass arm, and at all his players. When Enoch got hit by a pitched ball and thereby sent to his base, with Thatcher up, Mac senselessly yelled to him and tried to start the hit-and-run game, which he had a few moments before discarded. Enoch and Thatcher got confused, and finally when Thatcher hit into second both were easy outs in a double play.

Then the players, sore and disgusted, told Mac a few things. The little manager looked sick.

"I'm runnin' this team," he howled.

Chase suddenly confronted him with blazing eyes.

"No, you're not running the team. You're throwing away our chances. You've lost your head. Go soak it! Climb under the bench! Crawl through the fence! Anything—only get out!"

Mac fell back a beaten man. His eyes bulged, his lips moved, but no sound came forth. It was plain that he could not believe what he had heard. Chase, his find, his idol, his star, had risen against him.

"We'll win this game yet. Go hide somewhere, so we can't see your face. Mittie will run the team."

"Mittie!" echoed Mac. Then a spark of Chase's inspiration touched his smoldering baseball sense. Managers and players often do strange things; they follow blind leads and believe in queer omens. They are as superstitious as can be. Without a word Mac yielded to his impulse and left the bench.

Mittie-Maru jumped up into the vacated seat. A glow lighted his pale face; his beautiful eyes had a piercing, steely flash.

"Rube," he said to Poke, "cut the inside corner. Keep 'em high an' speed 'em up!"

The big knots stood out and rippled on the rail-splitter's arms. He was not lost to his opportunity. And there were friends and admirers from his native town there to see, to glory in his glory.

He struck out three successive Columbus hitters and the hopeless crowd took a little heart.

"What'll I do, Mittie?" asked Chase, picking out his bat.

"They're playing deep fer you. Dump one down third."

Chase placed a slow teasing bunt down the third base line and raced with all his speed for first. The play was not even close. It was his third hit.

Havil looked at Mittie. The new manager said, "Bunt toward first."

The second ball pitched, Havil laid down as if by hand along the first base line. Two on bases, no one out! The crowd awoke.

"Now fer mine, Mittie?" asked Benny.

"We'll try a double steal. It's not good baseball, but we'll try it. Swing wild on the ball an' balk the catcher. If the play goes through jest tap the next ball down in the infield."

207

Benny fell all over himself and all over the catcher. Chase drove into third and Havil reached second. The bleachers began to yell and stamp. As Ward got into motion with his swing Chase started home. It happened that the ball was a slow one, and Chase seemed to be beating it to the plate. Everybody gasped. Then Benny tapped the ball down in the infield and broke for first. The play bewildered the pitcher, catcher, and third baseman. Chase scored, Havil went to third, and Benny reached first.

Then the shrill cries, the whistles, the tin horns and clapping hands showed that the crowd had awakened fully to possibilities. Ford hit into deep short, who threw to second to catch Benny. The play was a close one, and Silk's decision favored the runner. Havil scored. Two runs scored, two men on bases, and nobody out! Roar on roar!

Through it all the little ragged hunchback sat coldly impervious. His fire raged deep. The years of pain and hopeless longing, the boyish hopes never to be fulfilled, had their recompense in that hour of glory. For victory shone in his piercing eyes. To a man, the players now believed in him, as boy, as manager, as genius, as baseball luck.

Speer bunted better than he hit, a fact of which Mittie took advantage.

"Lay one down to Wilson."

Wilson divined the play, came rushing in,

picked up the bunt with one hand, and made a splendid throw. One out, runners on second and third! Hicks was a poor hitter in a pinch, another fact Mittie remembered.

"Work a base on balls. Work hard, now!"

The contortions old man Hicks went through would have disconcerted most pitchers. Ward threw three balls for Hicks, then two strikes, and the next one, straight over, seemed a little high. Everybody gasped again.

"Four balls!" called Silk.

The crowd broke out afresh. One out, three runners on bases! Ziegler, batting for Castorious, hit a mean, twisting grounder between short and third. Both men went after it, knocked it down between them, but too late to catch the hitter. Another run scored, and the bases were full! How the bleachers screamed!

"Bing one, Cap!" said Mittie, from the heights.

Enoch met the first ball squarely. It sailed fast and true into the second baseman's hands. The runners had no chance to move.

"O-h-h! hard luck!" moaned the crowd.

"Never mind thet. Stick at 'em!" cried Mittie, jumping down from his perch. "A couple more hits an' the game's on ice. Dude, poke one to left. Don't swing. Jest poke one over the infield."

Thatcher went to bat while Enoch ran to the coacher's box and began to yell and screech, to tear up the grass with his spikes, to give every indication of insanity. Thatcher was remorselessly unanxious. He made Ward split the plate, and at last with three-and-two he placed a short fly back of third. Another runner scored.

Two out, bases full, one run to tie!

Mittie-Maru suddenly lost all his quiet; he jumped at Chase and clasped him with small, clawlike hands; his eyes shone on Chase with a power that was hypnotic. And through that gleam of power beamed his friendship and hope and faith.

"Chase, somethin' tol' me it would hang fire fer you! Now! Now! My Star of the Diamond, it's up to you. If ever in yer life you put the wood on one, do it now!"

When Chase hurried up to the plate, the great crowd rose and shouted one long sharp cry, and sank into intense waiting silence. The situation was too critical for anything but suspended breath.

Enoch's coaching pealed over the field.

"Oh! My! Mugg's Landin'! Irish stew! Lace curtains! Ras-pa-tas! We're a-goin' to do it! We can't be stopped now. Oh! My! They're takin' him out! They need another pitcher!"

The Columbus captain sent Ward to the bench and ordered out Henson, a lefthander. As he nervously rubbed the ball, Enoch broke loose again.

"Henson, look who's at the bat!" he yelled, in terrible tones. *"It's Chase! He's leadin' the league! Oh! Oh! My! Mugg's Landin'—!"*

If ever Chase felt like flint, the time was then. He heard nothing. He saw nothing but the pitcher. It seemed he called upon all his faculties to help his eyesight. His whole inner being swelled with emotions that he subordinated to deadly assurance.

Henson took his swing and sent up a fast ball. Chase watched it speed by.

"Ball!" called Silk.

Henson swung again. Chase got the range of the ball, stepped forward, and, with his straight, clean, powerful sweep, met it fairly.

"Bing!" It rang off like a bell.

The crowd burst into thunder. When Chase's liners started off so, only the fence stopped them. This one shot for the corner behind center field. For one instant everybody thought the ball was going over, but it hit a billboard and bounced back.

What a long, booming, hoarse and thrilling roar rent the air! Two runners scored, and Thatcher was coming fast. Then in the wild moment all grasped that Chase, with his wonderful fleetness, was gaining on Thatcher. His fair hair streamed in the wind; his beautiful stride swallowed up the distance. The center fielder got the ball and threw to Starke, who had run out to receive the throw. As Chase, now close to Thatcher, turned third, Starke lined the ball home.

Every heart was bursting; every eye was staring. The women were screaming, "Run, boy! Run, boy! Oh! run! run! run!" yet could not hear their own voices. The men were roaring. "On! On! On! A-h-h!"

The Findlay players leaped like warriors around a stake. Mittie-Maru ran toward the plate. Starke's great throw sped on! Thatcher scored!

"Slide, Chase, slide!" In one blended roar the whole crowd voiced a fear, awful at the moment.

Chase slid in a flash of dust across the plate, a fraction of time ahead of the ball. It bounded low, glanced off the catcher's glove, and struck Mittie, who whirled late, fairly on his hump. Poor Mittie went down as if he had been shot, spun around like a top, and lay still.

But few on the field saw this accident. The crowd had gone into a sort of baseball delirium tremens. Chase had made a home run inside the grounds, scoring four more runs! A thunderbolt out of the clear sky would have passed unnoticed.

Somebody carried Mittie into the dressing room. The game went on. Poke blanked the Columbus players inning after inning. The heart was taken out of them. Findlay won.

Before a weak, voiceless, shaken, dishevelled,

happy crowd the score went up: Findlay 11, Columbus 8.

Inside the dressing room the players grouped silently, with pale faces, around a space where a doctor worked over Mittie-Maru. A cold hand gripped their hearts. The doctor kept shaking his head and working, working; still the little misshapen form lay huddled in a small heap, the pale, distorted face showed no sign of life.

"Ah!" breathed the doctor, in sudden relief.

Mittie-Maru began to stir. He twisted, his narrow breast heaved, he moaned in pain, he broke into incoherent speech. Then, as consciousness fully returned, he lived over the last play he had seen.

"Steady—Chase, ole man—eagle-eye, now ole boy—lay back an' bing the next one—*oh-h!* Run, Chase! Up on yer toes! Now yer flyin'—make it a triple! Come on! Come on! Come on—on—on! *It's a homer! It's a homer! It's a homer!*"

SIXTEEN

LAST INNINGS

IT was Wednesday following the great Saturday game. Chase hurried to his room where he had taken Mittie after the accident. He found the lad sitting up, a little wan, but bright and expectant.

"All over, Mittie!" shouted Chase. "The season's over; the championship is ours; today was the last game, and the directors made it a benefit for the team. Terrific of them, wasn't it?"

"No more 'n square. The team's made barrels of money. Wot'd you do today?"

"Oh, made Mac sore, as usual."

"How?"

"Well, we smothered Mansfield in an inning or so, and then Mac wanted us to lay down, strike out, make the game short. Now I'd have to try to bing one, even if my life were threatened. So I caught one on the nose, and, by George! Mittie, I hit it over the fence, and the ball broke a window in Mrs. Magee's house. Mac'll have to pay damages. Say, but wasn't he sore!"

"Thet makes six homers fer you, Chase, on our

own grounds. An' you've had fourteen triples, an' only three doubles. It's strange 'bout thet. Most fellers git more doubles. But you're so dinged fast on yer feet that you'd stretch most any double into a triple. Gimme them long-liner triples fer mine!"

"Mittie, how're you feeling? How about the banquet tonight?"

"I'll go, you bet. I'd be out home long ago, if you hedn't made me promise to stay here."

"Mittie, I've had some ideas working in my mind the last few days, and now everything's settled. You're going to live with me."

"Am I—?" began Mittie rebelliously.

"Yes."

"I've got a tintype of myself spongin' on you here—"

"Not here, Mittie. I have bought that white cottage in the maple grove by the river. And I've had it all fixed up. It's now ready for the furnishings. In a few days I'll write to Mother and Will to pack their duds and come on. Maybe we won't surprise them! You'll come out there to live with us. There's a dandy little room next to mine and it'll be yours. You'll like Will, and you'll love Mother. She's the sweetest—"

"I ain't a-goin' to do it," cried Mittie in a queer, strangled voice. The old, resolute strength had gone from it.

"Yes, you are. I'm big enough to carry you out there and tie you if necessary. Then I've got another idea. You know that little alcove next to King's store? Well, there's one there. I've had a carpenter measure it, and he's going to build a wee little stand there. You and I are going into business—cigars, tobacco, candy, etc. I furnish capital, you manage affairs, we divide profits. Why, it's a gold mine! There's not a place of that kind in town. Everybody knows you; everybody wants to do something for you. Didn't you ever think of selling things? There's money in it."

"Chase, it'd—be—grand," said Mittie. "I'll do it—I'll— Chase, if you ain't the best ever! But haven't you—any idees fer yerself?"

Then Mittie-Maru, the defiant, the Spartan lad, the sufficient-unto-himself, the scorner of emotions, the dweller in lonesome places, covered his face and sobbed as might any of the boys whom he ridiculed. But his weakness did not last long.

"Chase, I'll be dinged if thet soak I got in the game Saturday hasn't give me softenin' of the brain," he said and smiled through his tears.

Chase had seen the light of that smile in his mother's eyes; and in the eyes of another of whom he must not think. For a moment a warm wave thrilled over him and he felt himself sway beneath its influence. He had done his best for his mother; he had done right by Marjory; he had waited and

216

waited. So he made himself think of other things—of the new home, of peace for his mother, of ambition for Will, of companionship with Mittie, of his opening career.

"Come, Mittie, we must fix up in style for the dinner tonight, and it's time we were at it."

When they reached the hotel Mac made a grab for Chase and beamed on him.

"Chase, old boy, sure things are comin' great. Cas goes to Cleveland fer a tryout. I've sold Benny to Cincinnati an' you to Detroit. Burke offered twelve hundred fer you on Saturday, but I held out fer fifteen. An' I got the check tonight. I promised you one-third if you hit .400, an' you've gone an' hit .416. Chase, thet's awful good fer a first season. You lead the league. An' tomorrow you git yer five hundred bucks. Burke wrote me to tell you he'd send the contract. He offers two thousand. So you're on, an' I'm tickled to death. I've made you a star an' you've made me a manager."

Somebody else made a grab for Chase. It was Judge Meggs, who congratulated him warmly. Then Chase, with Mittie-Maru hanging to his coat sleeve, was deluged in a storm of felicitations.

The banquet room, with its long decorated table, brought a yell from the hungry ballplayers. The waiters began moving swiftly to and fro; the glasses clinked musically; the noisy hum of conversation and jest grew steadily louder and gayer. There were fourteen courses and every player ate every course, except Benny, who got stalled on the unlucky thirteenth. Then chairs were shoved back and cigars lighted.

Judge Meggs, who was toastmaster, rose and spoke for a few moments, congratulating Findlay on her great ballteam, and the directors on their prosperous season, and the players on having won the championship. At the close he ended with a neat presentation speech.

Then before each player was placed a large colored box with a fitting inscription on the lid. Chase's was ".416." Enoch's was "Mugg's Landing." Benny's was "My Molly O." On Cas's was a terrible representation of a bulldog, with the name "Algy" above and below Cas's well-known "Wha-at?" And so on it went down the line.

Inside the boxes were the purses, shares of benefits, and presents from directors and from individuals. Chase won both the hitting and base-stealing purses, Cas the pitcher's, Enoch the fielder's. Each got a silver watch, a gold scarf pin and cufflink buttons. Each got cards calling for an umbrella, a hat, a Morris chair, and a box of candy. All received different presents from personal friends and admirers. Chase was almost overcome to find that Judge Meggs and other friends had that very morning furnished his cottage completely.

Then the toastmaster interrupted the happy buzzings and called on Mac. The little manager bounced up with shiny face; he lauded Findlay and its generous citizens; he raved about the baseball team; he spouted over Cas and Benny, and almost ended in tears over Chase.

"Gentlemen," said Judge Meggs, impressively, "we have with us tonight a remarkable ballplayer and good fellow. He has captained the team with excellent judgment; he has been a great factor in our victory. We have expected much of him and have not been disappointed. We expect much of him tonight. For surely a man with his wonderful command of language, his startling originality of expression, and his powers of uninterrupted, flowing speech, such as we are all so happily familiar with, will give us a farewell word to cheer our hearts through the long winter to come. Gentlemen, Mr. Enoch Winters."

Enoch rose as if some subterranean force had propelled him. His round red face and round owl eyes had their habitual expression of placid wisdom. But Enoch had difficulty with his vocalization. "Gennelmen," he began, and then it was evident his voice frightened him. "I—this— y'see—" he stammered, rolling up his tongue into his cheek to find his never-failing quid this time failing him. "Great honor—sure—I—we 'preciate—" Then the voluble coacher, the bane of pitchers and umpires, the terror of the inexperienced, stammered that something was "too full fer words" and sat down. Whether he said "stomach" or "heart" no one knew, but all assumed he meant the latter and roared their applause.

Judge Meggs, with a few fitting words, called upon Castorious; and Cas, he of the iron arm, iron heart, and voice, could not establish relations between his mind and his speech.

Judge Meggs said: "Gentlemen, we want to hear from our great second baseman, who, we are sorry to say and happy also, will not be with us next season. For he is going higher up. We have heard of a yet better stroke of fortune that has befallen him. In brief, we understand he has won from our midst one of Findlay's sweetest and best girls, and that the happy fulfillment of such good fortune is to be celebrated upon a day in the near future. We think he owes us something. Gentlemen, Mr. Benny Ross."

"No one ever had such friends!" cried Benny dramatically. "No one ever had such friends!"

And that was all he could say.

"Gentlemen," said Judge Meggs, "we have with us tonight a lad who came to Findlay empty-handed, yet who brought much. We shall watch his future as we have watched him develop here. And when he returns to Findlay to become one of her solid, substantial businessmen, we shall not forget when he was a Star of the Diamond. Gentlemen, Mr. Chase Alloway."

Chase managed to rise to his feet, but was utterly unable to respond. Emotion made him speechless. He smiled helplessly at Judge Meggs and sat down. The judge called upon several other players, and they too might as well have been dumb.

Then Mittie-Maru laboriously climbed upon his chair, and raised his strange, shrunken figure. He put his right hand to his breast and beamed upon the company.

"Mr. Toastmaster an' friends," began Mittie, "my worthy captain an' fellow players are too full fer utterance. Mebbe the sparklin' stuff in the long-stemmed glasses hes tongue-tied 'em. Somebody must thank all of you gentlemen fer this banquet, an' it's up to me. If the bases was full now we could feel sure of gittin' a hit, fer we're sure long on hits an' short on speeches.

"Fer the team I wanter say thet this is a gran' an' glorious occasion, thet Findlay is the finest town in the U.S., thet the directors an' supporters of the team are real sports an' good fellows, the best ever! This hes been a great summer fer us all, an' we've been happy. We're sorry it's over.

Baseball players hev to go from town to town an' part from each other an' kind friends. An' I'm sure none of us will ever forgit the fight we made fer the pennant an' the friends we made in good old Findlay."

Right warmly did all join in applause. Then, after a parting word from the judge, good nights were spoken, and the banquet to the championship team was over.

Before Chase went home he wrote a letter to his mother, and told her, as he was still boss of the family, and disposed to become more so in the future, she and Will were to come to Findlay. They were to dispense with all the old useless furniture and belongings, that would only have reminded them of past dark hours, and to come prepared for a surprise and future brightness.

Chase slept poorly that night, and kept Mittie-Maru awake, and in the morning got him out at an early hour to see the cottage. It seemed that a fairy's hand had been at work during the last forty-eight hours. The cottage was furnished from one end to the other, not poorly nor yet lavishly, but in a manner that showed the taste of a woman and the hand of a man. Chase felt that someone had read his mind. Who had guessed which was to be his mother's room, and Will's, and his own, and therein placed such articles as would best please each? So Chase learned in another way that

the needs of the human heart are alike in everyone.

That day he and Mittie loaded the pantry with
all manner of groceries. Then while Mittie went
out to his old home in the brick kiln to fetch the
few things he owned, Chase fitted up the little
room next to his. When Mittie saw it he screwed
up his face and sat gingerly on the little, white
bed.

"I'll be dinged if it ain't swell!"

After this, Chase would have it that Mittie
should go with him to a store and purchase a suit.
Mittie submitted gracefully, and after a trying
time in the store he produced a dilapidated pocketbook and began to count out the price marked
on the tag of the selected suit.

"No, you don't," said Chase, "this is on me."

"Mebbe you tho't I was busted," replied Mittie,
with a smile. "I ain't on my uppers yet, me boy.
Never was much fer style, but, now when the
time comes, I can produce."

Chase and Mittie were arguing the question
when the storekeeper said they must regard the
suit as a present, and refused to be paid.

"Wot t' 'll!" exclaimed Mittie. "Hev I ben hittin'
the pipe?"

The afternoon and evening were very long to
Chase. He slept that night from sheer exhaustion.
He was up with the sun, woke Mittie, whistled,

sang, and consulted his watch every few moments. The train he expected his mother and Will
on was due at ten o'clock. He packed his effects,
and sent Mittie for a wagon to take them to the
cottage. Then he went, hours before train time,
to the station, where he paced the platform. What
an age it seemed! At last he heard the train whistle, and he trembled. He ran to and fro. Suppose
they did not come! With a puffing and rumbling
the engine slowed up and came to a stop.

Only two passengers got off, and upon these
Chase swooped down like a hawk. He gathered
the little woman up in his arms and smothered
all her voice except "my Chase."

"Hello, Will! How about college, old boy?"

"You great, brown giant!"

And that was all. Chase bundled them into a
hack, and telling the driver where to go, he looked
at his mother and brother, so as really to see them.
How changed they were! His mother's face had
lost its weary shade. She was actually young and
pretty again. And Will—he was not the same at
all. Bells of joy rang in Chase's heart. Then he
began to talk and he talked like a babbling brook.
Baseball, the championship, his leading the
league, his sale to Detroit, his many friends, about
the certainty of Will's going to college—everything but where they were going. Then the hack
stopped.

Chase helped them out and, turning to the hackman, thanked him and held up a dollar.

"This's my treat," said the hackman, tipping his hat.

"Say, isn't my money any good around here?" demanded Chase.

"Your money's the same as counterfeit in Findlay. Good luck!" With a smile, the hackman turned his team and drove away.

"Chase, what a pretty place!" said his mother. "Do you board here?"

"Well, not yet. But I hope to."

Chase opened the front door and ushered them in. A bright fire crackled in the open grate.

"Mother, this is home."

Then for a brief space the three mingled tears with their happiness. And at last the mother raised her face with a flush.

"How I have worried—for nothing!"

Chase called up the stairway. "Mittie! Come down. We've company."

Then he whispered to them, "Mittie is my little friend of whom I wrote. He's a hunchback. If you look at his eyes you will never think of his deformity."

Mittie came down without reluctance, yet shyly. The new suit considerably altered his appearance; nevertheless, as always, he made a strange and pathetic little figure. He advanced a few steps, stopped and waited, with his fine eyes fixed gravely and steadily upon them.

"I am very glad indeed to meet my son's friend Mittie," said Chase's mother.

"My name's Mitchel Malone," answered Mittie, "an' I'm happy to know you an' Chase's brother."

"Mittie-Maru, he'll always be to me," said Chase. "Mother, he is going to live with us."

"I hev no home," replied Mittie to Mrs. Alloway's kind, questioning look. "My parents are dead. I never saw them."

Then followed the pleasant task of showing the cottage and grounds. The day passed like a happy dream. At sunset Chase slipped away from them and went down through the grove to the river.

He was rejoicing in the happiness of others. Yet now that his hopes were realities an unaccountable weight suddenly lay heavy as lead on his heart. He had succeeded beyond his wildest fancy. There was the cottage, and it contained his friend Mittie-Maru, and Will, with the clear light of joy in his eyes, and his mother, well, and happier than he had ever seen her. These were blessings such as he was sure he did not deserve, but humble and thankful as they made him, he was not entirely content. Suddenly the glamour of all he had been working to accomplish paled in the moment of its achievement.

The swift-flowing river murmured over stones and glided along the brown banks toward the setting sun. The song of the water was all the sound to break the silence. Silver clouds and golden light lay reflected in the river and slowly shaded as the sun sank. This hour with its diminishing brightness, its slow approach of gray twilight, its faint murmuring river song, sadder than any stillness, singularly fitted Chase's mood.

A shout from Mittie-Maru brought Chase out of the depths. He answered and turned toward the grove. Mittie came hobbling with a celerity that threatened peril to the frail limbs so unaccustomed to such effort.

"Lock the gate!" he called out, waving a letter at Chase.

"Wonder who's writing me?" asked Chase, failing to note Mittie's agitation.

"Thet's Miss Marjory's writin'."

Chase's hands trembled slightly. Mittie's eyes were gloriously bright.

"Last innin's!" sang out the lad. "You waited it out, Chase. An' now's the time to dig. Git up on yer toes an' run, Chase—run as yer never run turnin' third in yer life, an' when yer reach home base an' Miss Marjory, an' score—why—why just give her one fer Mittie, who umpired yer game."

Chase scarcely heard his little friend, and did

not see him hurry away toward the cottage, for his eyes were now fixed on the opened letter.

DEAR CHASE:

This letter is as difficult to write now as it has been to keep from writing sooner.

I have so much to tell you. Ever since you saved the Geyser well, Father has been on my side, and I persuaded him to take me to see the last Columbus–Findlay game.

He had forgotten he used to play ball when a boy, and it came back to him. First he grew excited, then red in the face, and he shouted till he lost his voice. Before the game was half over he turned purple. When you made that wonderful, wonderful hit he smashed a hole right through his hat.

Such a state as he was in when we got home! His hat was a wreck, his coat mussed, his collar wilted, and his face all crimson. But I never saw him so happy, and even Mother's disgust at his appearance made no difference.

I think—I am sure—we made life miserable for her. She said you might come to see me. And—I say come soon.

MARJORY.